"I found baby Demi right there." Fran pointed to the bushes in the corner. **"It's still totally unbelievable to me. Finding her alive so far away from the resort is one of those inexplicable miracles."**

Their eyes met. "Finding my niece alive in time to *save* her constitutes another miracle. That's *your* doing," Nik said in a deep voice full of emotion.

He hunkered down to examine the spot, fingering the bushes. After he stood up, he pulled out his cell phone and took several pictures. Before she could stop him he took a picture of her, then turned and snapped a few more of the back of the hotel.

"When Demi is old enough to understand, I'll show her these pictures."

He handed her the phone and his fingers overlapped hers, conveying warmth. She backed away far enough to get his tall, hard-muscled frame in the picture, with the garden just behind him.

As they went back into the hotel Nik ushered Fran inside the rear door. His touch might be impersonal, but she felt it in every atom of her body.

Physical attraction was a powerful thing. Under other circumstances she could be swept away. Thankfully she'd learned her lesson with Rob. Though he'd been conventionally handsome, she'd discovered good looks weren't enough to hold a relationship together, let alone a marriage.

For him to say he'd be willing to adopt and then change his mind had inflicted indescribable pain. Fran had not only lost hope of being a mother, she'd lost the ability to trust.

Dear Reader

Miracles come in so many assorted ways it would be impossible to name them all. When I thought about writing a set of stories about miracle babies my mind ran through a list of possibilities.

While I was pondering the exact one I wanted, I remembered seeing a news headline: 'Miracle Baby'. There was a picture of a baby, old enough to sit up, but you'll never guess where she was—*in the middle of a corn field* in the midwest portion of the US! Her parents had been killed in a tornado ten miles away. Instantly an idea for my novel sprang to mind, and I knew I had to write BABY OUT OF THE BLUE.

Remember, life is stranger than fiction.

Enjoy!

Rebecca Winters

BABY OUT OF
THE BLUE

BY
REBECCA WINTERS

First published in Great Britain 2013
by Mills & Boon, an imprint of Harlequin (UK) Limited.
Harlequin (UK) Limited, Eton House, 18-24 Paradise Road,
Richmond, Surrey TW9 1SR

© Rebecca Winters 2013

ISBN: 978 0 263 23421 3

Harlequin (UK) policy is to use papers that are natural, renewable and recyclable products and made from wood grown in sustainable forests. The logging and manufacturing process conform to the legal environmental regulations of the country of origin.

Printed and bound in Great Britain
by CPI Antony Rowe, Chippenham, Wiltshire

Rebecca Winters, whose family of four children has now swelled to include five beautiful grandchildren, lives in Salt Lake City, Utah, in the land of the Rocky Mountains. With canyons and high alpine meadows full of wildflowers, she never runs out of places to explore. They, plus her favourite vacation spots in Europe, often end up as backgrounds for her romance novels, because writing is her passion, along with her family and church.

Rebecca loves to hear from readers. If you wish to e-mail her, please visit her website: www.cleanromances.com

Books by Rebecca Winters:

THE COUNT'S CHRISTMAS BABY
ACCIDENTALLY PREGNANT!
THE NANNY AND THE CEO
HER DESERT PRINCE
AND BABY MAKES THREE
HER ITALIAN SOLDIER
A BRIDE FOR THE ISLAND PRINCE
THE RANCHER'S HOUSEKEEPER

CHAPTER ONE

FRAN MYERS' GAZE fastened on the scenery unfolding at every bend along the coastal road. Against the azure blue of the Aegean, the miles of white beaches with their background of deep green pines didn't seem real. Dark, fast-moving clouds swirled overhead, adding a dramatic aspect to the landscape. The panorama of colors was quite spectacular.

"I didn't know the Greek Riviera was this beautiful, Kellie. I'm in awe. It's so unspoiled here."

"That's why my husband had built the resort where we'll be staying for the next few days. The Persephone is the latest getaway for the very wealthy who can afford to have peace and quiet in total luxury."

It was such a fabulous area, the news didn't surprise Fran. "Is that why you've brought me all the way from Athens? Because you think I need peace and quiet?"

"Exactly the opposite. Many royals come here to vacation. I'm hoping you'll meet one who's unattached and gorgeous. You two will take one look at each other and it'll be love at first sight."

"That'll never happen, not after my bad marriage."

Fran's best friend since childhood flashed her a searching glance.

"Don't look so surprised, Kellie."

"I'm not surprised. What I see is that a vacation for you is long overdue. Every time I've called since your divorce, you've been at the hospital doing your patient advocacy work all hours of the day and night, and you couldn't talk more than a few minutes. You need a passionate romance to bring you back to life!"

"You're hilarious. It's true I've buried myself in work to keep me from thinking, but it's been a year. I'm doing a lot better now."

"Liar. I don't need your mom to tell me you don't have a life and need to take a break in completely different surroundings. I intend to see you're pampered for a change. We'll laze around, swim, sail, hike, do whatever while we scope out eligible men."

"You're incorrigible, but I love you for it. You know very well that when I told you I would come, I didn't expect you to go to this kind of trouble for me. I thought we'd be staying in Athens to see the rest of the sights I missed when I flew over for your wedding. That was too busy a time to get everything in. Besides, your adoring husband couldn't be thrilled with this arrangement."

Kellie waved her hand in the air in a dismissive gesture. "July is Leandros's busiest time. He's off doing business in the Peloponnese and looking for new resort sites in other places. This is the perfect time for me to spend with the person who's been the sister I never had. That's why I called you to come now and wouldn't take no for an answer. We have a lot of catching up to do."

"Agreed."

The two women had been friends since they'd attended the same elementary school in Philadelphia. They could read each other's moods. Having gone through the good and the bad of their lives together, they'd become closer than most sisters.

When they'd been planning this trip, they'd talked about September. But Kellie had changed her mind and was insistent on Fran coming as soon as possible. Something was going on; normally her friend traveled everywhere with her husband. It sounded as though she needed to talk to Fran in person.

Two years ago Kellie had married millionaire Greek business tycoon Leandros Petralia in Athens. Fran had been the matron of honor at her wedding. Though they'd talked on the phone and emailed since then, they'd only seen each other the half a dozen times Kellie had flown home to Pennsylvania to be with her family for a few days. On those short visits Fran could tell her friend was so crazy over her exciting husband, she couldn't bear to be gone from him longer than a few nights.

But clearly that wasn't the case today. Kellie seemed wired, and her show of gaiety was somehow artificial. Physically she was thinner than the last time Fran had seen her. On their five-hour drive to the resort south of Thessolonika, Kellie's glib responses throughout their conversation weren't at all like her.

Fran decided to hold off until tomorrow to have a heart-to-heart with her golden-blonde friend. Right now she wanted Kellie to concentrate while she drove the fabulous slate-blue luxury saloon—too fast for Fran's liking. As they whizzed along, Fran's eyes darted to the stormy sky. "Have you noticed how black those clouds ahead are?"

"Yes. It's almost spooky and so windy, it's buffeting the car. That's very strange. This place is legendary for its sunshine. Wouldn't you know it would choose today to cloud up for your arrival?"

"Maybe it's a bad omen and your hubby came back to Athens early only to find you missing."

"Don't be absurd—" Kellie answered with uncharacteristic sharpness. "He's got his secretary with him. Maybe they're really somewhere in the Dodecanese Islands, a favorite place of his when he wants to relax."

With Mrs. Kostas? She was in her late forties.

Her friend's emotional outburst took Fran by surprise. "I was just having some fun with you." She'd never seen Kellie explode this way before.

"I'd rather talk about you. Has Rob called yet, wanting you two to get back together?"

"No. In fact, I've heard he's involved with someone at his work."

"He'll soon realize he's lost the best thing that could ever happen to him."

"Spoken like my best friend."

Kellie had been the maid of honor at Fran's wedding. Four years ago Fran had married Rob Myers after meeting him through mutual friends in Philadelphia. He was an upcoming estate-planning attorney working for a prestigious local law firm. On their third date she'd told Rob that she could never conceive, so if he didn't want to see her again, she'd understand.

He'd told her he didn't have a problem with adoption. It was a great option for childless couples. Besides, he was interested in *her*, and he had proven it by marrying her. After a year passed, she'd brought up the idea of putting in adoption papers, but he'd said it was too soon to think about and kept putting her off.

Eventually she realized he had issues and she suggested they go for counseling so they could talk about them in depth. But the counseling revealed that with the busy law practice thriving, he no longer had the time or the interest to enlarge their family, especially when the child couldn't be their own flesh and blood. Fran was enough for him.

But she wanted children badly. After three years of a married life no longer happy or fulfilling for either of them, they'd agreed to divorce. It was the only way to end the pain. Since then Fran had decided marriage wasn't for her. Kellie scoffed at such nonsense and told her she would find the right husband for her no matter what.

"Kellie? I don't know about you, but I'm thirsty. Let's stop at the village I can see up ahead and get ourselves a drink at one of those cute hotel bars."

"It's only twelve more miles to the Persephone," her friend responded in a clipped tone. "We'll order room service and have dinner in our suite where we can relax. But, of course, if you can't wait…"

"I hope you don't mind."

Kellie's hands tightened on the steering wheel, further proof her friend was barely holding herself in check. "Of course not."

There was no softening of her tone, or a reassuring smile. Right now, Fran was more concerned with Kellie, who'd been driving over the speed limit. She never used to drive this fast. After they stopped for a soda maybe Fran could prevail on her friend to let her drive the rest of the way. She'd use the pretext that she'd never been behind the wheel of a Mercedes before.

Fran wanted both of them to arrive at the resort in one piece. With this wind, the driving could be dangerous. To her alarm, the idea came into her head that Kellie wasn't even seeing the road. Intuition told her the once flourishing Petralia marriage was having problems.

Not Kellie, too.

By the time they reached the village proper the wind was so powerful there was actual debris in the air. "Stop in front of that hotel on the corner, Kellie. It's starting to hail. Let's make a run for it."

The small ice balls pounded down, emptying the street of people rushing to take cover. All the shops and cafés had taken their display items and tables inside. When Fran entered the hotel bar with Kellie, tourists and staff alike were huddled in groups talking and gesticulating while they brushed themselves off.

"Kellie? You understand Greek. What are they saying?"

"I don't know, but I'll find out."

Fran followed her friend over to the counter where Kellie got a waiter's attention. He rattled off an answer to her question. She turned to Fran. "Someone in the back was listening to the radio and heard that tornado-like winds have swept through the area. There's no television reception right now. The police have issued a warning that everyone should stay indoors until the danger has passed. It's a good thing you wanted to stop here."

Considering the violence of the elements, it was providential they'd been passing by this village. "Let's get a drink and find a place to sit down while we wait this out."

After being served, they carried their sodas to an

unoccupied bistro table. By now the hail had stopped and a heavy downpour had descended.

Kellie frowned. "I can't believe this weather."

"Since it made the six o'clock news, maybe you ought to call and let Leandros know you're all right."

Her jaw hardened. "He knows. Whenever I leave our apartment, my bodyguard Yannis follows me. If my husband is interested, he'll phone me." She pulled out her cell and checked everything. "Nope. No calls yet. See?" She showed her the screen. "No messages."

"Kellie—" Fran put a hand on her friend's arm. "Tell me what's going on. I'd planned to wait until morning to ask you that question, but since we won't be leaving here any time soon, I'm asking it now. I want to know what's happened to the happiest wife I've ever known. Where did she go?" The reason Kellie had wanted Fran to come to Greece was no longer a mystery.

Kellie averted her soulful brown eyes. "Maybe you should be asking Leandros that question."

"He's not here. *You* are. What's wrong?"

Kellie's face was a study in pain. "I'm losing him, Fran. In fact, I've discovered I never really had him and I can't stand it."

Her friend's emotions were so brittle they'd crack if Fran pushed too hard. Instead of arguing with her that it couldn't possibly be true, she took a deep breath before saying, "Does this have anything to do with the fact that you haven't gotten pregnant yet? You're probably putting too much pressure on yourself to give Leandros a child. These things take time."

"Since I've been diagnosed with seminal plasma hypersensitivity, that's the understatement of the year.

I've never wanted to talk about it, but you deserve an explanation.

"Our marriage took a crushing blow when I discovered that the painful itching and hives I experienced after intercourse was because my body is allergic to Leandros's sperm. When the doctor told me twenty thousand-plus women suffer from it in the U.S. alone, I couldn't believe it."

Fran shook her head. "I had no idea."

"I know. Growing up, I never knew such a problem existed. Leandros had to have been devastated, but he was wonderful about it. He's worn a condom every time, but I *know* deep down he must hate it.

"The doctor knew we wanted a baby and said we could try artificial insemination with a good hope of success. They have to wash his sperm of the proteins first before the procedure is done. We've been trying that method since last year, but unfortunately it hasn't worked for us. He said he's willing to adopt. How's that for irony after what you've lived through? At this point I'm thinking it's just as well," came the bleak admission.

Fran couldn't believe what she was hearing. "What do you mean?"

"I'm talking about Karmela Paulos. She came to work for Leandros a month ago as part of the typing pool."

Ah. Karmela. The woman couldn't get to him by other means, so she'd insinuated herself into the office. Now things were starting to make sense.

Karmela Paulos was the gorgeous, raven-haired younger sister of Leandros's first wife, Petra. Petra had been pregnant when she'd died in a helicopter crash over the Ionian Sea.

Two years later Leandros had met Kellie by accident at the Cassandra in Athens, one of the famous Petralia five-star hotels. It hadn't taken long before he'd married her, but it seemed that since his late wife's funeral, Leandros had acquired a constant companion in Karmela who was always around.

Fran had met her at the wedding and hadn't liked her proprietorial behavior with Leandros either. Though he was now a husband for the second time, it seemed Karmela had won herself a position that placed her closer to Leandros than before. This was foul play at its best. Being her brother-in-law, he could hardly turn her down.

"It was clear to me at the wedding that your marriage had thwarted her dreams to become the next Mrs. Leandros Petralia." Whatever subterfuge was going on here, Fran was positive Karmela was behind it in order to break them apart. She clearly still wanted Leandros for herself.

Too bad. Fran intended to make sure this was resolved before she went back to Pennsylvania in two weeks.

"Tell you what, Kellie. You heard the warning from the police, so I have an idea. Since we're not supposed to be out on the street, how about we get a room for tonight right here?"

"That sounds good."

"I think so, too. It'll be fun. How long has it been since we hung out in some cozy little hotel like this?"

"I don't remember."

"We'll watch the news on TV when it comes back on, and we'll get some food. Then we can talk all night if we want. I've got an idea about how to thwart Karmela without your husband realizing what's happening."

"I don't know if that's possible."

Fran smiled. "You haven't heard my plan yet." She got up from the table. "I'll talk to the proprietor and arrange a room for us. When the rain stops, we'll go out to the car for our luggage."

By now Fran figured Kellie's bodyguard would have contacted Leandros wherever he was and told him his wife was safe and sound. She hoped Leandros would call her soon. The problems in their marriage were tearing her best friend apart. No one knew what that felt like better than Fran.

Nik Angelis had just entered his Athens penthouse when one of his brothers phoned him. He clicked on. "Sandro? What's up?" They'd already spent part of the day in a board meeting at the Angelis Corporation. Nik had recently taken over for his father who'd retired.

"Turn on your television. The news about the tornado is on every station."

"I was in it, remember?" It was the only talk at Angelis headquarters. After he'd seen his sister and her family off to Thessalonika early that morning on the company jet, Nik had headed over to the international air cargo station to check on some shipments. While he was talking business with one of the staff, a funnel had dropped down from clouds descending on Athens. It had swept through in a northwest direction and headed straight for the air cargo station.

After a few minutes it dissipated, but in that amount of time, it had caused damage to the constructions in its path and left a trail of destruction. Fortunately every-

one involved had escaped injury, including Nik. Before
he instructed his limo driver to take him to his office,
he'd made contact with his pilot.

Relief had filled him to learn they'd been at cruising
speed and out of range of the severe turbulence of the
weather pattern before the tornado had formed. Knowing his sister's family were safely on their way north
for a vacation, he'd been able to relax.

"No, no," Sandro cried anxiously. "Not that one. I'm
talking about another one that touched down near Thessalonika a few minutes ago."

Another one?

"Let's pray Melina and Stavros are safe."

Nik's heart had already received one workout this
morning, but now it almost failed him. "Hold on." He
raced into his den and clicked on the TV with the remote. Every station was covering the news using split
screens to show the funnel clouds of both tornadoes.

...and then another tornado struck a part of the
Greek Riviera at 5:13 p.m. this evening. It was re-
ported as a T-4, and has since dissipated, but we
won't know the true extent of the damage for a
while. Word has already reached the station that a
dozen villas and some private suites at the world-
famous Persephone Resort owned by the Petralia
Corporation, have been destroyed.

Nik felt as if a grenade had blown up his insides. The
Persephone was where Melina, Stavros and their infant
daughter were going to stay for the first two nights of
their vacation. Nik's good friend, in business and so-
cially, Leandros Petralia, was the owner of the resort.

"I called Melina on her cell, but there's no phone service." Sandro sounded frantic.

The knowledge sent ice through Nik's veins.

So far twenty people are unaccounted for. We repeat, it doesn't mean those are fatalities. Relief is pouring in from all over. We ask people to stay away from the area and let the police and search-and-rescue workers do their job. Cell phones are not working. We've posted a series of hotline numbers on the screen in case you have or need information about a loved one.

Pure terror seized his heart. "Do you think Cosimo is home from the office yet?"

"I don't know, but I'll try to reach him."

"Tell him to meet us at the airport, Sandro." He wanted both his brothers with him. "We'll fly to Thessalonika."

"I'm on my way!"

Nik clicked off, then phoned his driver and told him to bring the car around. On his way out the door he called his pilot and told him to ready the jet for another flight to Thessolonika. In a little over an hour Nik and his brothers could be there. They would need a car.

En route to the airport he phoned his parents at the family villa on Mykonos. They'd just heard the news and were in total anguish. "Our precious Melina, our Demitra," his mother half sobbed the words.

"Their suite may not have been among the ones affected, *Mana*. In any case, Stavros will have protected them. We have to have faith. Sandro and Cosimo are going to fly there with me now. You get on one of those hotlines and see what you can find out! Call me when you know anything. Let's pray phone service is restored there soon. I'll call you when I know anything."

A rap on the hotel-room door the next morning brought both girls awake. With the TV knocked out last night, they'd talked for hours about Karmela. Before falling asleep, Fran had made sure her friend was armed with a firm plan in mind for once their vacation was over.

Kellie lifted her head and checked her watch. "It's ten after ten!"

"Maybe it's one of the maids waiting to make up our room. I'm closest." Fran jumped out of bed in her plaid cotton pajamas. "Who is it?" she called through the door.

"Yannis."

"I'll talk to him," Kellie murmured. In an instant she slid out of her bed and rushed over to the door. The dark-haired bodyguard stood in the hall while they spoke in Greek. The conversation went on for a minute until Kellie groaned and closed the door again. Her face had turned ashen.

Fran thought her friend was going to faint and caught her around the shoulders. "What's wrong? Come sit down on the chair and tell me."

But Kellie just stood with tears gushing down her pale cheeks. "A tornado touched down twelve miles to the north of here last evening, killing nine people. Among them were five guests staying at the P-Persephone."

They stared at each other in disbelief. "I can't credit it," Fran whispered in shock. "If we hadn't pulled over when we did…" They could have been among the fatalities. She started to tremble.

"Yannis said Leandros heard about it on the television, but he was almost a thousand miles away in Rhodes. He flew here immediately, but even with his own jet and a police escort, he had trouble getting into the site until the middle of the night. Three of the twelve individual suites were demolished. There's nothing left of them."

Fran gasped. "On top of the human tragedy, your poor husband is having to deal with that, too."

"Leandros told Yannis it's a nightmare, and there's still no phone, internet or television service to that area. He got hold of him through the help of the police to let me know what has happened. I've been asked to stay put here until he joins us. Yannis said it shouldn't be long now." Kellie's teeth were chattering.

"Come on. We need to get ready and go downstairs. Knowing your husband, he must be absolutely devastated and is going to need you more than he's ever needed anyone in his life." Now would be the time for Kellie to draw close to Leandros and put the plan they'd talked about last night into action.

Both of them showered and dressed in a daze. Fran put on white linen pants with a spring-green-and-white-printed top. She tied her dark honey-blonde hair back at the nape with a white chiffon scarf. After slipping on white sandals, she announced she was ready. Nothing seemed real as they packed up and carried their bags downstairs to wait for Leandros.

To Fran's surprise, the main doors of the hotel were open for patrons to walk out and enjoy coffee at the tables set up in front of the building. Warm air filtered inside and a golden sun shone out of a blue sky. Up and down the street, life appeared to be going on as usual. You would never have known there'd been a natural disaster twelve miles away from here last evening.

A waiter approached them. "The tables in front are full. If you'll walk around to the patio in back, we'll serve you out there."

"Thank you," Fran said before taking Kellie aside. "Yannis is sitting outside in his car by yours. Let's stow our luggage and then tell him we'll be in back of the hotel. We need breakfast with our coffee. He can show Leandros where to come. I feel like soaking up some sun until he arrives. Don't you?"

"I guess so," Kellie answered in a wooden voice.

They walked over to their car and put their cases in the back. "This hotel seems to be a popular place. Go ahead and talk to Yannis while I get us a table before they're all taken."

"Okay."

Fran followed the stone pathway to the rear of the hotel where blue chairs and tables were set with bright blue-and-white-check cloths. There was an overhang of bougainvillea above the back door, and further on, a small garden. Too bad the wind had denuded most of the flowering plants. There were only a few red petals left.

She took a seat in the sun while she waited, thinking she was alone. But all of a sudden she heard a strange sound, like a whimper. Surprised, Fran looked around, then up. Maybe it was coming from one of the rooms on the next floor where a window was open.

Again she heard the faint cry. It didn't sound frantic and it seemed to be coming from the garden area. Maybe it was a kitten that had been injured in the storm.

Poor thing. She jumped up and walked over to investigate.

When she looked in the corner, a gasp escaped her lips. There, on its back in the bushes, lay a dirty black-haired baby with cuts from head to toe—

Fran couldn't fathom it. The child was dressed in nothing more than a torn pink undershirt. The little olive-skinned girl couldn't be more than seven months old. Where in heaven's name had she come from? A groan came out of Fran. She wondered how long the child had been out here in this condition.

Trying to be as gentle as possible, Fran lifted the limp body in her arms, petrified because the baby had to be dying of hypothermia. Her pallor was pronounced and her little lids were closed.

"Fran?" Kellie called out and ran up to her. "What on earth?"

She turned to her friend with tear-filled eyes. "Look— I found this baby in the garden."

A gasp flew from Kellie's lips. "I can see that, but I can't believe what I'm seeing."

"I know. Quick—get me a blanket and drive us to the hospital. I'm afraid she's going to die."

Kellie's eyes rounded before she dashed through the back door, calling in Greek for help. Within seconds, the staff came running out. One of them brought a blanket. Fran wrapped the baby as carefully as she could and headed around the front of the hotel. Kellie ran ahead of her to talk to Yannis.

"He'll drive us to the hospital."

He helped Fran and the baby inside the backseat of his car. She thought he looked as white-faced as Kellie, who climbed in front. She looked back at Fran. "What do you think happened?"

"Who knows? Maybe the mother was on the street around the corner when a microburst toppled the stroller or something and this dear little thing landed in the garden."

"But she's only wearing a torn shirt."

Both of them were aghast. "I agree, nothing makes sense."

"Do you think she could have been out there all night?"

"I don't know," Fran's voice trembled. "But what other explanation could there possibly be, Kellie? The baby has superficial cuts all over."

"I'm still in shock. You don't suppose the mother is lying around the hotel grounds somewhere, too? Maybe concussed?"

"It's a possibility," Fran murmured. "We know what tornadoes can do. The one in Dallas tossed truck rigs in the air like matchsticks. Sometimes I feel that's all we see on the news back home. I just have never heard about a tornado in Greece."

"They get them from time to time. Leandros told me they usually happen near coastal waters."

The baby had gone so still, it was like holding a doll. "Tell Yannis to please hurry, Kellie. She's not making any more sounds. The police need to be notified and start looking for this baby's parents."

Once they reached the emergency entrance, everything became a blur as the baby was rushed away. Fran wanted to go with her, but the emergency-room staff told her they needed information and showed her to the registration desk.

The man in charge told them them to be seated while he asked a lot of questions. He indicated that no one had contacted the hospital looking for a lost baby. Furthermore, no mother or father injured in the storm had been brought in. So far, only a young man whose car had skidded in the downpour and hit a building had come in for some stitches on his arm.

When the questioning was over he said, "One of our staff has already contacted the police. They've assured us they'll do a thorough investigation to unite the baby with her parents. An officer should be here within the hour to take your statements. Just go into the E.R. lounge to wait, or go to the cafeteria at the end of the hall."

When they walked out, Kellie touched Fran's arm. "I think we'd better eat something now."

"Agreed."

After a quick breakfast, they returned to the E.R. lounge. "If the baby lives, it will be thanks to you and your quick thinking. Had you been even a couple of minutes later arriving at the patio the baby might not have had the strength to cry and no one would have discovered her in time."

Hot tears trickled down Fran's cheeks. "She has to live, Kellie, otherwise life really doesn't make sense."

"I know. I've been thinking the same thing." They both had. Kellie had been praying to get pregnant and it had been Fran's fate not to be able to conceive. What a pair they made! She found two seats and they sat down.

"I wish Leandros would get here. After seeing this baby, I'm worried sick for what he's had to deal with. Lives were lost in that tornado. He'll take their deaths seriously."

"It's too awful to think about. I'm still having trouble believing this has happened. When I saw her lying in those bushes, I thought I was hallucinating."

Before long, two police officers came into the lounge to talk to them. There was still no word about the parents. After they went out again, Fran jumped up. "I can't sit still. Let's go into the E.R. Maybe someone at the desk can tell us if there's been any news on the baby yet."

Kellie got to her feet. "While you do that, I'm going outside to talk to Yannis. Maybe he's heard from Leandros."

Quickly, Fran hurried through the doors to the E.R. and approached one of the staff at the counter. "Could you tell me anything about the baby we brought in a little while ago?"

"You can ask Dr. Xanthis, the attending physician. He's coming through those doors now."

Fran needed no urging to rush toward the middle-aged doctor. "Excuse me—I'm Mrs. Myers. I understand you might be able to tell me something about the baby my friend and I brought to the hospital." Her heart hammered in fear. "Is she going to live?"

"We won't know for several hours," he answered in a strong Greek accent.

"Can I see her?"

He shook his head. "Only family is allowed in the infant ICU."

"But no one has located her family yet. She's all alone. I found her in the bushes in the garden behind the hotel."

"So I understand. It's most extraordinary."

"Couldn't I just be in the same room with her until her parents are found?"

The man's sharp eyes studied her for a moment. "Why would you want to do that?"

"Please?" she asked in a trembling voice.

"She's a stranger to you."

Fran bit her lip. "She's a baby. I—I feel she needs someone," her voice faltered.

All of a sudden a small smile lifted one corner of his mouth. "Come. I'll take you to her."

"Just a moment." She turned to the staff person. "If my friend Mrs. Petralia comes in asking for me, please tell her I'm with the baby, but I'll be back here in a little while."

"Very good."

The doctor led her through the far doors to an elevator that took them to the second floor. They walked through some other doors to the nursery area where he introduced her to a nurse. "I've given *Kyria* Myers permission to be with the baby until the police locate the mother and father. See that she is outfitted."

"This way," the other woman gestured as she spoke.

"Thank you so much, Dr. Xanthis."

His brows lifted. "Thank you for being willing to help out."

"It's my pleasure, believe me."

CHAPTER TWO

FRAN FOLLOWED THE NURSE to an anteroom to wash her hands. She was no stranger to a hospital, having worked in one since college to follow up on patients who needed care when they first went home.

When she'd put on a gown and mask, they left through another door that opened into the ICU. She counted three incubators with sick babies. The baby she'd found in the garden was over in one corner, hooked up to an IV. She'd been fitted with nasal prongs to deliver oxygen. A cardiopulmonary monitor on her chest tracked the heartbeat on the screen.

She was glad to see this hospital had up-to-date equipment to help the baby survive, yet the second she spied the little form lying on her back, so still and help-less, she had to stifle her cry of pain. The precious child had cuts everywhere, even into her black curls, but they'd been treated. Mercifully none of them were deep or required stitches. With the dirt washed away, they stood out clearly.

The nurse pulled a chair over so Fran could sit next to the incubator. "Everyone hopes she will wake up. You can reach in and touch her arm, talk to her. I'll be back."

Finally alone with the baby, Fran studied the beautiful features and profile. She was perfectly formed, and to all appearances had been healthy before this terrible thing had happened to her. All the cuts and hookups couldn't disguise her amazingly long black eyelashes or the sweetness of her sculpted lips.

With such exquisite coloring, she looked like a cherub from the famous painting done by the Italian artist Raphael, but this cherub's eyes were closed and there was no animation.

She put her hand through the hole and touched the baby's forearm. "Where did you come from? Did you fall out of heaven by accident? Please come back to life, little sweetheart. Open your eyes. I want to see their color."

There was no response and that broke her heart. Even if the baby could hear her, she couldn't understand English. "Of course you want your mommy and daddy. People are trying to find them, but until they do, will you mind if I stay with you?"

Fran caressed her skin with her fingers, careful not to touch any cuts. "I know you belong to someone else, but do you know how much I'd love to claim a baby like you for my own? You have no idea how wonderful you are."

Tears trickled down her cheeks. "You can't die. You just can't—" Fran's shoulders heaved, but it wouldn't do for the baby to hear her sobs. By sheer strength of will she pulled herself together and sang some lullabies to her.

After a time the nurse walked over. "I'm sure you're being a comfort to her, but you're wanted down in the E.R. Come back whenever you want."

Fran's head lifted. She'd been concentrating so hard

on the baby, she hadn't realized she'd already been up here several hours. "Thank you."

"Leave everything in the restroom on your way out."

"I will." With reluctance she removed her hand and stood up. "I'll be back, sweetheart."

A few minutes later she reached the E.R. lounge and discovered Kellie talking quietly with Leandros. Her attractive husband had arrived at last, but he looked as though he'd aged since Easter. When he'd flown to Pennsylvania with Kellie in the Petralia company jet at that time, the three of them had gone out for dinner and all had been well.

The second her friend saw her, she jumped up from the chair and ran across the room to meet her. Leandros followed. "Is the baby going to make it?" Kellie cried anxiously.

"I don't know. She's just lying there limp in the incubator, but she's still breathing and has a steady heartbeat. Have the police found her parents yet?"

"There's been no news."

Leandros reached for her. "Fran—" he whispered with a throb in his voice. It revealed the depth of his grief. They gave each other a long, hard hug.

"It's so good to see you again, Leandros, but I wish to heaven it were under different circumstances. I'm so sorry about everything," she told him. "I'm sure you feel like you've been through a war."

He nodded, eyeing his wife with pained eyes. Something told Fran the pain she saw wasn't all because of the tragedy. She could feel the negative tension between Kellie and her husband. Her friend hadn't been exaggerating. In fact, their relationship seemed to be in deeper trouble than even Fran had imagined.

"Five guests at the resort died," he muttered morosely. "We can thank God the honeymoon couple weren't in their suite when the tornado touched down or there would have been two more victims. Unfortunately the other two suites were occupied. Mr. Pappas, the retired president of the Hellenic Bank and his wife, were celebrating their sixtieth wedding anniversary."

"How terrible for everything to end that way. What about the other couple?" Fran asked because she sensed his hesitation.

Leandros looked anguished. "The sister of my friend Nikolos Angelis and her husband had only checked in a few hours earlier with their baby."

"A baby?" she blurted.

"Yes, but when the bodies were recovered, there was no sign of the child. The police have formed a net to search everywhere. You can imagine the anguish of the Angelis family. They're in total shock. People are still combing the area."

"Nik is the brilliant youngest of the Angelis brothers," Kellie informed her. "He's the new CEO of the multimillion-dollar mega corporation established by their family fifty years ago. He was out of the country when Leandros and I married, or he would have been at the wedding."

"I remember seeing some pictures of him in a couple of magazines while I was on the plane flying over." *Gorgeous* was the only word to come to mind.

Leandros nodded. "We've both put up money for volunteers to scour the region, but so far nothing. His parents are utterly devastated. They not only lost their daughter and son-in-law, but their little granddaughter."

Granddaughter?

The mention of a baby girl jolted her as she thought of the baby upstairs fighting for her life.

"How old is the baby?"

"Seven months."

"What color is her hair?"

"Black."

A cry escaped her lips.

Maybe she hadn't fallen out of heaven.

Was it possible she'd been carried in the whirlwind and dropped in the hotel garden? Stranger things had happened throughout the world during tornadoes.

"Kellie?"

"I know what you're thinking, Fran—" Kellie cried. "So am I." The two women stared at each other. "Remember the little girl in the midwest a few years ago who was found awake and sitting up ten miles away in a field after a tornado struck, killing her entire family? We both saw her picture on the news and couldn't believe it."

"Yes! She was the miracle baby who *lived*!"

"It would explain everything."

Leandros's dark brows furrowed. "What are you two talking about?"

"Quick, Kellie. While you tell him what we're thinking, I'm going back upstairs to be with the baby. Maybe she has come to by now. After hearing from Leandros that their baby is missing, I think she could be that lost child! She *has* to be! There's no other explanation. She *has* to live." Those words had become Fran's mantra.

The police had made a grid for the volunteers to follow. Nik and his brothers had been given an area to cover in the pine trees behind the resort. They'd searched for hours. Separated by several yards, they walked abreast while looking for any sign of Demi.

Debris had been scattered like confetti, but he saw nothing to identify their family's belongings. The tornado had destroyed everything in its path, including lives. Pain stabbed him over and over.

Where in the hell was the baby? How could they go home without her body and face their parents? The grief was beyond imagining.

Each of his brothers had two children, all boys. Their wives and families, along with Stavros's family had flown to Mykonos to join Nik's parents. He knew Sandro and Cosimo were thanking providence that their own children hadn't been anywhere near either tornado, but right now their hearts were so heavy with loss, none of them could talk.

Demi was the only little girl in the family, so beautiful—just like her mother. Not having married yet, Nik had a huge soft spot for his niece. She possessed a sweetness and a special appeal that had charmed him from the moment she was born.

Melina's baby was the kind of child he would love to have if he ever settled down. But that meant finding the kind of woman who could handle what he would have to tell her about himself before they could be married.

Up to now he hadn't met her yet and was forced to put up with the public's false assumption about him. Throughout the last year, various tabloids had put unauthorized pictures of him on their covers with the label Greece's New Corporate Dynamo—The Most Sought-After Playboy Bachelor of the Decade. He was sickened by the unwanted publicity. But this tragedy made the problems in his personal life fade in comparison.

Just two weeks ago he'd bought Demi a toy where you passed a ball through a tube and it came out the other end. She loved it and would wait for it to show up, then crawl on her belly after it. She could sit most of the time without help and she put everything possible in her mouth. Her smile delighted him. Never to see it—or her—again…he couldn't bear it. None of them could.

Hot tears stung his eyes at the thought that the seven-month-old was gone, along with her parents. It was a blow he didn't know whether he could ever get over. He and Melina had shared a special bond. She'd been there for him at the darkest point in his life. A grimace broke out on his face as he realized he couldn't even find her baby. He felt completely helpless.

Sandro caught his arm. "We've finished this section."

"Let's move to the next grid."

"Someone else has done it," Cosimo muttered.

"I don't care," he bit out. "Let's do it again, more thoroughly this time. Examine every tree."

They went along with him. Maybe five minutes had gone by when his cell phone rang. He checked the caller ID. "It's Petralia."

Their heads swiveled around, as they prayed for news that some volunteer had found her body.

"Leandros?" he said after clicking on. "Any word yet?"

"Maybe. If you believe in miracles."

Nik reeled. "What do you mean?"

"I'm with my wife at the hospital in Leminos village. It's twelve miles south of you. Come quickly. This morning her best friend Mrs. Myers from the States, who's staying with us for a few weeks, found a baby girl, barely alive, in a hotel garden."

Nik's hand tightened on the cell phone. "Did I just hear you right?"

"Yes. If you can believe this, she was lying in some bushes at the rear of the hotel. On their drive to the Persephone yesterday, the storm got so bad, they ended up staying in Leminos."

"You mean your wife and her friend—"

"Could have been among the casualties," he finished for him. The emotion in Leandros's voice needed no translation. "Fran went out to the back patio to get them a table for breakfast when she heard some faint cries and walked over to investigate."

"What?"

"It's an absolutely incredible story. The child is cut up and bruised. All she had on was a torn undershirt. They brought her to the hospital and Fran has been staying in the infant ICU with her in order to comfort her. So far no parents have shown up yet to claim her."

"You've *seen* her?" Nik cried out.

"Yes. She's about seven months old, with your family's coloring. She's alive, but not awake yet. So far that's good news according to the doctor who thought at first they were going to lose her. Come as fast as you can to the E.R. entrance. We'll show you to the ICU."

He eyed his brothers. "We're on our way, Leandros— My gratitude knows no bounds."

"Don't thank me yet. This child might not be your niece."

"I have to believe she is!"

Nik clicked off and he and his brothers started running through the forest. On the way he told them the fantastic story. Before long they reached the rental car at the police check point. Nik broke every speed record getting to Leminos while they all said silent prayers.

Once they reached the village, he followed the signs to the hospital. Leandros and his wife were waiting for them in the lounge of the E.R. His lovely wife, Kellie, was in tears over what had happened to Nik's family. He was deeply moved by her compassion. She, in turn, introduced them to the doctor who was taking care of the baby.

"Come with me and we'll see if she belongs to you." On the way upstairs the doctor said, "I'm happy to report that a half hour ago, the baby opened her eyes for the first time and looked around. I think that had something to do with *Kyria* Myers who's been singing to her and caressing her through the incubator. She's the one who first heard the baby cry and found her before she lost consciousness."

Nik couldn't wait to see if the baby was Demi, but he understood they had to wash their hands and put on masks and gowns. It took all his self-control not to burst into the ICU. If it wasn't their niece lying in there it would kill all three of them to have to return to Mykonos without her.

When they were ready, the nurse opened the door and beckoned them to follow her to the corner of the room. A woman gowned and masked like themselves sat next to the incubator with her hand inside the hole to touch the baby. With her back to them, he could only glimpse dark honey-blond hair tied back with a filmy scarf. She was singing to the child with the kind of love a mother might show for her own flesh and blood.

Touched by her devotion to a child she didn't even

know, Nik had a suffocating feeling in his chest as he drew closer and caught his first sight of the baby.

"Demi—"

His brothers crowded around, equally ecstatic at discovering their niece lying hooked up to machines, but squirming as if she didn't like being trapped in there. She kept turning her head. Sounds of joy and tears escaped their lips as her name echoed through the ICU. But Demi took one look at them and started crying. With their masks on, she was frightened.

The woman caressing her limbs spoke in soothing tones and soon calmed her down. Nik could hardly believe it. Those words might be spoken in English, but Melina's baby responded to the tender tone in which she'd said them.

After a minute, the woman pulled her hand through and stood up. Nik noticed she was of medium height. When she turned to them, he found himself staring into eyes a shade of violet-blue he'd only seen in the flowers that grew in certain pockets on Mykonos. They were glazed with tears.

"Mrs. Myers? I'm Nik Angelis," he spoke through the mask. "These are my brothers Sandro and Cosimo. I understand you're the person we have to thank for finding our niece before it was too late to revive her."

"I just happened to be the first guest to walk out to the back patio of the hotel to be served," came her muffled response. "When I heard her crying, I thought it was a kitten who'd been injured by the storm. I almost fainted when I saw her lying there face-up in the bushes." Her eyes searched his. "What's her name?"

"Demitra, but we call her Demi."

"That's a beautiful name." He heard her take a deep

breath. "There's no way to express how sorry I am for the loss of your sister and her husband, Mr. Angelis. But I'm thankful you've been reunited with their daughter. She's the most precious child I've ever seen," she said with a quiver in her voice. Nik happened to agree with her. "If you could remove your masks, I'm sure it would make all the difference to her."

"Demi doesn't seem to have any problem with *you* wearing one."

He saw a distinct flush creep above her mask. "That's because I've been talking to her since we brought her here. I couldn't stand it that she didn't have anyone to give her love. Babies want their mothers. Her experience had to have terrified her."

Not every woman had such a strong maternal instinct as Melina's, but being a married woman, he had to assume Mrs. Myers had children of her own. "Leandros told me you're here on vacation. For you to forget everything except taking care of Demi constitutes a generosity and unselfishness we appreciate more than you could ever know. She'll be the reason our parents can go on living."

"It's true," his brothers concurred before expressing their gratitude.

Nik moved closer. "I hope you realize our family owes you a debt we can never repay."

She shook her head. "What payment could anyone want except to see that sweet little girl reunited with her family?" Her eyes still possessed a liquid sheen as they played over him. "Anyone can see she's an Angelis from head to toe. Of course I don't know about the noses and mouths yet." Her husky voice disturbed his senses in ways that surprised him.

In spite of the horrendous grief of the past twenty-four hours, her comment made one side of his mouth lift. Until he'd entered the ICU and watched the loving way she was handling Melina's daughter, he couldn't imagine ever having a reason to smile again.

She took a step back. "Well—I'll leave you gentlemen alone to be with your niece. When you speak to her, your voices will be blessedly familiar and will reassure her."

Nik wasn't so certain Demi wouldn't start to cry the second Mrs. Myers left the room. "Where are you going?"

"Downstairs to join Kellie."

"Don't leave the hospital yet. We need to talk."

"Since I'm their guest, I'm not sure what our plans are now."

Making one of those decisions on sheer instinct in case she got away, he said, "In that case, I'll go downstairs with you. I need to call our parents and give them the kind of news that will breathe new life into them. Above all, they'll want to thank you." He turned to his brothers and told them his plans before he left for the anteroom with her.

Once inside, he removed his mask and gown while she untied hers. Though she was married, he was a man who enjoyed looking at a beautiful woman and was curious to see what she looked like unwrapped.

Once she'd discarded everything, he discovered a slender figure clothed in a stunning green-and-white-print outfit. She had classic bone structure and a face that more than lived up to the beauty of her eyes. In a word, she stole his breath.

"What's the verdict?" he asked after she'd studied him back.

Again, he saw warmth enter her cheeks, but she didn't look away. "I happened to see your picture on the cover of a magazine while I was reading on the plane." Nik's teeth snapped together at the mention of it. "If you want honesty, then let me say I'm glad your niece received all the feminine features of her parentage."

He'd been expecting her to say something about his reputation. Instead her thoughts were focused on Demi. Her surprising comment lightened his mood.

"Your sister must have been a real beauty to have produced a daughter like Demi."

Nik reached for his wallet and showed her a picture. "This was taken on Melina's thirtieth birthday two months ago. She and Stavros had been trying for four years for a baby before one came."

Kellie needed to hear that. Not every woman conceived as quickly as one hoped.

Fran studied it for a moment. "What a lovely family." Her voice shook. "I see a lot of your sister in her."

His throat swelled with raw emotion. "Yes. She'll live on through Demi." He opened the other door. "Shall we go downstairs?"

"I'll ride down with you," Dr. Xanthis said. "We'll need confirmation of your relationship to the baby with a DNA test."

"Of course. I'll ask the hospital in Athens to send my information so you can run a test."

"Excellent. I'll tell the lab to expedite the process."

Fran wondered what condition had been serious enough to put Nik in a hospital and to have provided a

DNA match, but it was none of her business. She wished she weren't so aware of him.

Though she'd always thought Leandros was a true hunk, Nikolos Angelis was in a class by himself. Despite the grief lines etched in his striking Greek countenance, he was easily the most attractive male she'd ever met in her life. The photos of him didn't do him justice.

Besides his masculine appeal, he had the aura of a man in charge of his life—one who could accomplish anything. Kellie's hope that Fran would meet some gorgeous royal on this trip and fall instantly in love was still laughable, but she had to admit Nik Angelis was a fabulous-looking man.

Standing next to him, Fran thought he must be at least six feet three of solid lean muscle. She wasn't surprised he was still wearing soiled suit trousers and a creased blue shirt with the sleeves shoved up to the elbows. All three brothers had arrived in clothes they'd worn to work when they'd heard about the tornado. Naturally they'd dropped everything to fly to Thessalonika to search for their family. None of them had slept.

He needed a shave, but if anything, his male virility was even more potent. She noticed he wore his black wavy hair medium length. It had such a healthy gloss that it made you want to run your hands through it. Before the door opened, Fran gave him another covert glance.

Brows of the same blackness framed midnight-brown eyes with indecently long black lashes like Demi's. Between his hard-boned features and compelling mouth, she had to force herself to stop staring. Until now, no men she'd worked around for the last year had made any kind of an impact.

To be singling him out when he'd just been hit with the loss of his sister and brother-in-law made her ashamed. She rushed from the elevator ahead of him. But just as she was about to turn toward the lounge, he grasped her elbow. A warm current passed through her body without her volition.

"Come outside with me where my cell phone will work better. My parents will want to ask you some questions."

"All right."

They walked through the sliding doors into the late-afternoon sun. It was quarter to five already. She watched and listened as he communicated in unintelligible Greek with his parents. During the silences, she read between the lines. Her heart went out to all of them.

After a few minutes his penetrating gaze landed on her. He handed her the phone. "They speak English and are anxious to hear anything you can tell them."

Fran took the cell phone from him and said hello.

"We are overjoyed you found our Demitra," his mother spoke first in a heavy Greek accent. In a voice full of tears she said, "Our son tells us you've been at the hospital with her the whole time."

"Yes. She's the sweetest little thing I ever saw. A cherub. And now that she's awake, she seems fine."

"Ah… That's the news we've been waiting to hear," Nik's father broke in. "We want to meet you. I told him to bring you and the Petralias to Mykonos when Demitra is released. After the funeral, you will stay on as our guests for as long as you wish. He tells me you've just started your vacation. We'd like you to spend it with us. Because of you, a miracle has happened."

"Someone else would have found her if I hadn't, Mr.

Angelis, but thank you very much for your kind words. Here's Nik." She handed him the phone. "I'm going to the lounge," she whispered.

"I'll be right there." His deep voice curled through her as she walked back inside the building.

Once again she found Kellie and Leandros seated on one of the couches. You didn't have to be a mind reader to guess they were having an intense conversation that wasn't going well. Judging by Kellie's taut body and his grim countenance, they were both in agony. But when they saw Fran, they stopped talking and stood up.

Kellie rushed over to her, as if she were glad for the interruption. "Dr. Xanthis came to talk to us a minute ago and said he'll release the baby tomorrow once the DNA testing is done. I was just telling Leandros that since she's been reunited with her family, you and I can continue on with our vacation while he flies back to Rhodes."

Obviously Kellie wanted Fran to fall in with her wishes despite anything Leandros had to say. But her comment caused his firm jaw to tighten, making Fran uncomfortable. "My project supervisor can finish up the work there. I have a helicopter waiting to fly the three of us back to Athens. One of my employees will drive the car home."

Kellie tossed her blond head. "Don't be silly, Leandros. I don't want to interfere with your work. Besides, Fran and I want to sightsee in places where we've never been before."

"Where exactly?" he demanded quietly. Fran had never heard him so terse.

"We're going to do some hiking, but haven't decided

all the details yet. After dinner, we'll get out the map to plan our next destination."

Just when Fran didn't think she could stand the tension any longer, Nik entered the lounge and walked up to them. He darted her a searching glance. "Did you tell them about my father's invitation?"

The girls exchanged a private look before Fran said, "I haven't had time yet." Kellie's troubles with Leandros had weighted them down.

In the next breath Nik extended them all a personal invitation to fly to Mykonos in the morning and spend a few days with his family. "My parents insist."

"I was planning to pay them a personal visit anyway, Nik. We'd be honored to come," Leandros spoke up before Kellie could say anything. "Under the circumstances, I'll drive us back to Athens in Kellie's car. Tomorrow we'll fly to your villa."

Uh-oh. That meant a lot of hours for them to talk, but Fran decided that was a good thing. Kellie could approach him with the plan they'd talked about last night.

"Excellent." Nik shot Fran a level glance. "I realize you came here on vacation, but if it wouldn't inconvenience you too much, would you mind staying with me at the hospital overnight?

"Between the two of us taking turns, we ought to be able to comfort Demi while my brothers arrange for Melina's and Stavros's bodies to be flown home on our company plane. I'd very much like your help when we take Demi in the helicopter to Thessalonika airport in the morning. From there we'll fly on the plane to Mykonos."

Her heart thudded. Nik honestly wanted her help with his niece? He couldn't know she wasn't ready to say goodbye to the adorable child. Another night to hold her thrilled Fran to pieces.

Trying to sound in control she said, "If you feel it's necessary, I'd be glad to help." She looked at Kellie, knowing her friend didn't want to be left alone with her husband right now. The situation was precarious. "What do you think, Kellie? Would it be all right with you?"

Fran knew Kellie was stuck in a hard spot. She couldn't say no to Nik who'd already lost part of his family, but that meant she'd have to face Leandros sooner than she'd expected. It was providential they'd come up with an idea last night. *It had to work!*

"Of course. I'll see you tomorrow and we'll resume our vacation."

If Kellie worked things out with Leandros, maybe she wouldn't want to go on a trip after all. Fran was hoping for that outcome. "All right then."

The news seemed to relax Leandros a little. No doubt he was thankful for this much of a reprieve so he could talk to his wife. "Fran? I'll bring your bags in from the car."

Nik shook his head. "Don't bother, Leandros. I'll come with you and put them in my rental car." He turned to Fran. "I'll be back in a minute."

After the two men walked out of the lounge, Fran put an arm around Kellie's shoulders. "I'm sorry about this. I had no idea Nik would ask me to stay on. Frankly, I didn't know what to say."

"Neither of us had a choice. It would have been churlish to refuse him."

"If I stay overnight with the baby, are you going to be okay?"

Her friend took a shuddering breath. "I thought I'd

have two weeks to be away from Leandros, but this situation has changed things for the moment and can't be helped. Wish me luck broaching your suggestion to him," she whispered in a pain-filled voice.

"Kellie, last night we talked a lot about Karmela, but I sense there's still something you haven't told me. What is it?"

Her head was bowed. "I was afraid to tell you. N-night before last, I told him this vacation was more than that. I wanted a separation."

Fran groaned. "No wonder he looks shattered." Fran was aghast that their marriage had already broken down to that extent.

Her friend's lips tightened. "He said I wasn't thinking clearly before he stormed out of the bedroom angrier than I've ever seen him. On our drive back to Athens, I'm going to do what you said. I'll tell him that since I haven't gotten pregnant, I need something substantial to do and want to work with him in his private office. I'll remind him I was once a part of an advertising agency and am perfectly capable.

"But if he turns me down flat, and I'm afraid he will, then he needs to hear what I think about the sacred Karmela. Up until now I've been careful about saying anything negative, but no longer. I might as well get everything out in the open right now."

Fran would have told her not to plunge in with Leandros where Karmela was concerned yet. Let the idea of his wife working with him take hold first. But both men came back in the lounge, preventing further conversation.

Leandros put his arm around his wife. "It's going to be a long drive. We need to get going."

"I'll see you tomorrow." Fran hugged her. "Tell him you love him so much, you want the opportunity to work with him," she begged in a quiet whisper. "I don't see how he can turn you down."

When Kellie let her go without an answer, Leandros grasped his wife's hand and they walked out of the lounge.

She felt Nik's gaze on her. "We need a meal. Let's drive to the hotel where you stayed last night and get a couple of rooms so we can shower and have dinner. By then we'll feel much more prepared to spend the night with Demi."

"That sounds good to me." She would have said more, such as the fact that he hadn't had any sleep last night, but she'd bring it up to him later.

He walked her out to the parking lot and helped her into the rental car. His dark eyes noticed every detail, and she was glad she was wearing her linen pants. Once he got in the driver's side he said, "You'll have to guide me to the hotel."

"It's on the southern end of the village near the main highway." She gave him a few directions, not quite believing that he was taking her to the place where she'd found his niece. "There on the corner," she said. He flipped a U-turn and pulled up close to the front entrance where people were dining. "Before we go in, I'll show you the garden out in back."

"Good. I want to take pictures while there's still some light."

She got out of the car before he could help her and they walked around the side to the rear of the hotel where more customers were enjoying their evening meal. Fran kept going until she came to the garden.

"I found her right there." She pointed to the bushes in the corner. "There's no indication she lay there all those hours. It's still totally unbelievable to me. Finding her alive so far away from the Persephone is one of those inexplicable miracles."

Their eyes met. "Finding her alive in time to *save* her constituted another miracle. That's *your* doing," Nik said in a deep voice full of emotion.

He hunkered down to examine the spot, fingering the bushes. After he stood up, he pulled out his cell phone and took several pictures. Before she could stop him, he took a picture of her, then turned and snapped a few more of the back of the hotel. "When Demi is old enough to understand, I'll show her these pictures."

"Let me get one of you standing there," she said on impulse. "Demi will be thrilled to see her uncle in the very place she landed. She'll always be known as the Greek version of Dorothy Gale, the girl from Kansas in *The Wizard of Oz.* But instead of being blown to Oz, Demi was caught up in a tornado and deposited in a Grecian garden miles away. What a ride she must have had," her voice throbbed.

Something flickered in those black-brown depths. "Amen," he said before handing her the phone. His fingers overlapped hers, conveying warmth. She backed away far enough to get his tall, hard-muscled frame in the picture with the garden just behind him.

As she finished and gave the phone back to him, the proprietor approached. "You're the one who found the miracle baby!"

"Yes. And this is Nikolos Angelis, the baby's uncle. I was just showing him where I discovered her."

The owner stared at Nik. "You are the new head of

the Angelis Corporation. I saw your picture on television."

"That's right," he murmured.

Fran said, "His sister and her husband were killed in the tornado, but the baby survived and will be leaving the hospital tomorrow. I'll ask them to return the blanket to you."

"Not to worry about that. We are all very sorry about this tragedy, *Kyrie* Angelis."

Nik shook the man's hand. "Thank you."

"Can we serve you dinner? It will be our pleasure."

"We'd like that, wouldn't we, Mrs. Myers?" The way he included her as if they'd been friends a long time seemed to come out of the blue. Her pulse raced for no good reason.

"Come through to the front desk and everything will be arranged," the owner said.

"We'll need two rooms to change in. Later my brothers will be arriving to stay the night."

"Very good."

Nik ushered her inside the rear door. His touch might be impersonal, but she felt it in every atom of her body.

Once behind the desk, the owner gave them each a key. "The rooms are on the second floor."

"Thank you." Nik turned to her. "Why don't you go on up while I bring in our bags? I always keep one onboard the plane in case of an emergency. With a change of clothes and a good meal, we ought to be set to spend the night with Demi."

She nodded and hurried up the stairs. It was hot out and she was eager for another shower. He wasn't far behind with her suitcase. After walking into her bedroom, his gaze found hers. "I'll meet you in the back of the hotel in half an hour. After we eat, we'll take our bags out to the car and leave for the hospital."

"Demi must be so frightened."

He grimaced. "My brothers promised to stay with her until we get there. She knows and loves them. That ought to help."

Her eyelids stung with unshed tears. "But she'll still be looking for her mommy and daddy."

He lounged against the doorjamb. "Of course, but I wouldn't be surprised if she isn't looking for *you* too. See you shortly."

Fran averted her eyes. *He was too striking.*

Physical attraction was a powerful thing. Under other circumstances, she could be swept away. Thankfully she'd learned her lesson with Rob. Though he'd been conventionally handsome, she'd discovered good looks weren't enough to hold a relationship together, let alone a marriage.

For him to have said he'd be willing to adopt and then change his mind had inflicted indescribable pain. Fran had not only lost hope of being a mother, she'd lost the ability to trust.

CHAPTER THREE

AFTER A PHONE CALL to the hospital in Athens, Nik showered and shaved. Once they'd eaten a good meal, he felt restored and imagined Mrs. Myers did, too. He'd almost slipped and called her Fran in front of the proprietor, but realized he needed to keep thinking of her as Mrs. Myers, a married woman.

En route to the hospital, he phoned Sandro who told him the doctor had moved Demi to her own room in the pediatric wing. They didn't have to wear masks and gowns any longer and were able to hold her.

"That's wonderful," Fran declared when he'd conveyed the good news to her. "After what she's been through, she needs to be cuddled."

Nik's thoughts exactly. He parked around the side entrance to the hospital with easier access to the pediatric unit.

On the drive over he'd inhaled his companion's flowery fragrance. By the time they got out of the car and entered the hospital, he could hardly take his eyes off her stunning figure clothed in a summery print skirt and white blouse. She wore white leather sandals. With her hair flowing to her shoulders from a side part, she made an enticing vision of femininity he doubted she was aware of.

He thought about her being in Greece on her own. American women had a tendency to be independent. For her and Leandros's wife to be traveling alone shouldn't have surprised him. But he thought Fran's husband a fool to let his attractive wife vacation in a foreign country without him.

He wondered how Leandros handled being apart from his wife, but he had no right to speculate. The media had painted Nik to be the most eligible playboy in Greece, a label he was forced to wear. But it would do as a cover to hide his real reason for not being married by now. Therefore he wasn't in any position to judge what went on in another man's life or marriage.

In truth he felt shame for having any of those thoughts where Mrs. Myers and Kellie Petralia were concerned. If the two women hadn't been out together, Fran wouldn't have spotted their precious Demi. That was a miracle in and of itself. So was her desire to make sure the baby hadn't been left alone at the hospital.

Interesting that it had been Fran, not Kellie, who'd planted herself next to Demi in the ICU. He wondered why…

For a moment Nik's thoughts flew to Lena, the last woman he'd dated. After two dates she'd suggested they move in together. She was a desirable woman, but he didn't believe in living together. Because of a painful issue from his past that had prevented him from proposing to any woman yet, he didn't want to encourage her. In order not to be cruel, he'd stopped seeing her.

In truth, none of his romantic relationships had ever gotten past the point where he'd felt he could take the next step. As for Lena, he couldn't help wondering what would have happened if she'd been the one who found Demi. Would she have dropped everything and changed her plans in order to comfort the baby? Would she have shown such a strong maternal instinct?

He doubted it, yet the minute he'd posed those questions, he chastized himself. It wasn't fair to compare any of the women in his past to Fran. The moment she'd discovered Demi in that garden, she'd felt a special responsibility to care for her. The whole situation was unlike any other. She was unique, but his thoughts had to stop there. She was another man's *wife*. He needed to remember that before he got in real trouble.

What did he mean by *before?* He already was in trouble, because deep in his gut, he felt she was the kind of woman he might trust enough to reveal his painful secret to. Why her and why now?

Following his brothers' directions, he found Demi's room. When he walked inside with Fran, he saw an exhausted-looking Cosimo walking around holding the baby, but she was fussing. Sandro had passed out in an easy chair brought in for them.

Nik nodded to his brother and walked over to take the baby from him, needing to nestle her against his chest. He was still incredulous she was alive. She recognized him, but there was no accompanying smile because she wasn't herself. Her world had literally been blown apart.

"It's me, Demi, your Uncle Nikolos. I'm here." He kissed her neck and cheeks, careful not to hurt the cuts that were already healing. "Where's my little sunshine girl? Hmm?" But she still seemed restless, the way she'd been with Cosimo.

Fran walked up next to him and touched her black curls. "Hi, Demi. Do you remember me? It's Fran."

The baby heard her voice and turned her head to focus on her. All of a sudden she started to cry and held out her arms to Fran, almost leaping to get to her. Nik couldn't believe a bond had formed so fast that his niece would go to Fran with an eagerness that was astonishing. Even more amazing was the way Demi settled down and buried her face in Fran's neck, reminding him of the way she always was with Melina.

Fran rocked her and sang a little song. Nik took advantage of the time to take Cosimo aside and talk to him. "I've got rooms for you and Sandro at the hotel where Fran found the baby." He gave him the directions. "Take Sandro with you and get some sleep. Come back here tomorrow morning and we'll use the hospital helicopter to get to Thessalonika before we fly home. The bodies should be loaded on the plane by then."

Sadness filled Cosimo's eyes. "You're sure you won't need help?"

"Positive. Fran and I will take turns tonight."

"She's willing to stay?"

Nik nodded. His brother looked relieved. "But you haven't had any sleep."

"I'll get it now."

"I'm afraid Demi hasn't slept. She's looking for Melina. I've never felt so helpless in my life."

"I have a feeling she might get her rest now that Fran is here. You two go on."

Cosimo nodded and woke up their brother. Nik walked them out of the room and down the hall. After saying goodnight, he went to the desk where he asked for a cot to be brought in.

Within a few minutes, housekeeping delivered one and left. Finally he was alone with Fran and turned off the light. Though he was beyond tired, he still wanted to talk to her before he got some sleep. Heaving a deep sigh, he sank down in one of the chairs and sat back, marveling over her rapport with his niece.

"I think you've gotten her to sleep."

"Yes," she whispered. "The dear little thing must be so tired and bewildered."

"With you holding her, it's apparent she'll get the rest she needs. When you're too tired, I'll take over."

"I'm not desperate for sleep like you. Kellie and I slept in until ten this morning. Why don't you undo the cot and lie down? I'll waken you when it's your turn."

"Promise?"

She gave him a half smile. "Believe it."

In the semidarkness, her generous mouth drew his attention, spiking his guilt for having those kinds of thoughts about her. "Where did you come from?"

"Not from the whirlwind, if that's what you mean," she drawled.

He crossed his legs at the ankles. "You might as well have. Earlier today my brothers and I were combing through the pines behind the resort, dying a little with every step because there was no trace of Demi.

"Then the call came from Leandros telling us to get to the Leminos hospital as fast as possible because a miracle may have happened. Suddenly, out of nowhere, I find this American woman taking care of my niece as if she were her mother. I'm still not sure if I'm dreaming this or not."

Fran kissed Demi's curls before sitting down in the other chair. "Then we're both having the same inexplicable dream. Day before yesterday I flew from Philadelphia to Athens to spend my vacation with Kellie. Leandros had already flown to Rhodes on business.

"At six yesterday morning, she and I left the city because we knew we had a long drive ahead of us. We'd planned to drive around new areas of Greece neither of us had visited before. She wanted me to see the Petralias' latest resort, so we decided to stay a night at the Persphone before moving on.

"But by late afternoon a fierce storm arose and I suggested we pull off the highway in Leminos to find shelter. Kellie wanted to keep going because the resort was only twelve miles farther, but then the hail started, so we hurried inside the first hotel we came to.

"When we learned from the staff that a tornado had destroyed some suites at the Persephone, we both fell apart. Not only because we realized we might have been caught and lost our lives, too, but because she knew Leandros would be devastated to think such a thing had happened to the guests staying at the resort. He would take it very hard and he was so far away on business. There was no way to reach him by phone."

Nik sat foward. "For a while it was chaos. Do you know about the other tornado?"

Her beautiful eyes widened. "What are you talking about?"

"There was one at the airport yesterday morning."

"You're kidding!"

He shook his head. "I came close to being affected. After seeing my sister and her family off around 6:30 a.m., I went over to the air cargo area to do business when a funnel cloud struck. No one was injured, but it was terrifying to see how much damage it did in the space of a short time."

"Now I understand why it was so windy when we left, but we haven't had any news here."

"That's not surprising. I was just leaving my office at the end of the day when my brother phoned and told me about a second tornado."

"We get so many in the States, but I didn't realize you got them, too."

"Once in a while," he murmured, "but yesterday's phenomena probably won't happen for another couple of decades or more."

"Let's pray not."

"When I turned on the TV, what I heard was enough to make my blood run cold." Just the way he said it made her chill. "My brothers and I took off in the plane for Thessalonika. By the time we reached the resort, we learned that Melina and Stavros were two of the victims. To our horror, there was no sign of Demi."

"I don't know how any of you are holding up." The sadness in her voice touched him to the core.

"It's our parents we're worried about. That's why it's so important you come to the villa with me tomorrow. They love their grandchildren, but Demi has a special place in their hearts because she's the only girl."

"I can understand that." Fran looked down at Demi who was cuddled in her arms, fast asleep. "This little child is too precious for words. She'll always be a special joy to them."

"And to me."

A tremor rocked his body. On Melina's birthday, she'd taken Nik aside and asked him to be Demi's guardian if anything ever happened to her and Stavros.

Without hesitation he'd told her yes, but he was unable to entertain the thought of anything ever happening to his sister and her husband. Remembering her request, the hairs lifted on the back of his neck. Had she asked him because of a premonition?

"Demi's blessed to have such loving family."

Nik eyed Fran speculatively. "Since you're married and have such a close rapport with my niece, I'm wondering if you have children."

She didn't meet his eyes. "No."

No?

"How does your husband let you leave him for such a long time?" The question he'd sworn not to ask left his lips before he could stop it.

"We're divorced."

His thoughts reeled. "How long ago?"

"A year."

What husband in his right mind wouldn't have held on to a woman like her? Nik sensed he'd be wandering into forbidden territory with more questions, yet he was intrigued by her. Now that he knew those pertinent facts, he was determined to learn more and no longer felt guilty about it. With time and patience, he'd get his answers. "Are you ready to let me hold her now?"

"I'm fine. I was going to suggest you go to sleep."

"Maybe I will for a little while."

He got to his feet to undo the cot. After taking off his shoes, he stretched out. Another heavy sigh escaped him. "This feels so good, I fear I might never get up again. You're sure you don't mind?"

"Positive. Holding this angel is a joy. You need sleep or you won't be any good to your family tomorrow."

"You're right. If I haven't said it already, I'm grateful you're here for Demi."

"*I'm* the one who's grateful."

His instincts told him those weren't empty words. He needed to find out what emotions were driving them, but before he could ask, oblivion took over.

The next time he was aware of his surroundings, it was morning.

Nik sat up and got to his feet, removing the blanket Fran must have thrown over him. His gaze shot to her. She was asleep in the easy chair while Demi slept in the hospital crib.

He had no idea how long Fran had stayed awake, but she'd chosen not to disturb him for any reason. Unable to help himself, he looked down, studying her facial features. With no makeup and her dark blond hair somewhat disheveled, she was lovelier than most women who worked at it all day.

Since Demi was still asleep, he tiptoed out to the hall to phone his brothers. They were on their way over with a new outfit for the baby. As he talked with them, the doctor slipped inside the room. By the time Nik hung up and returned, he discovered Fran standing by the crib talking to the doctor. She'd brushed her hair and applied lipstick, looking amazingly fresh for someone who'd probably been up most of the night.

The doctor turned to him with a smile. "The lab has confirmed she's your niece. I'm happy to say her cuts are starting to heal. She's doing fine in every regard and can be released. Keep her hydrated. What she needs now is the love of her family which I can see isn't going to be a problem. Just so you know, the media has been inundating the hospital for information.

"In order to make them go away, I gave a statement that I hope will satisfy them and give your family a chance to breathe before they descend on you. When you're ready to leave, come to the desk and someone will escort you to the roof where the helicopter is waiting."

Nik shook his hand. "Thank you for everything you've done, doctor. The Angelis family is indebted to you."

The older man's eyes flashed. "And no doubt to *Kyria* Myers who made the baby feel safe and loved until you arrived. We could use more like her around the ICU." He eyed Fran. "Are you a nurse?"

"No. But I work in a hospital for patients' rights and make certain they get the follow up care they need after they go home."

"You wouldn't like a job with us, would you?" he threw out.

"I've already got a position in mind for her," Nik inserted, flashing her a glance. She looked at him in confusion. "Of course I haven't discussed it with her yet."

The thought had been percolating in his mind since yesterday, but until he knew she was divorced, he'd kept it at bay. Before he could explain more, the doctor said, "I'll be at the desk. When you're ready to leave, I'll escort you to the private elevator that will take you to the roof." He left as Nik's brothers arrived with a new quilt and stretchy suit they'd purchased.

All the talking woke up Demi who turned to the bars and tried to get up. She babbled and looked longingly at Fran, asking to be rescued. Everyone chuckled as Fran leaned over and plucked her from her prison. Giving her a kiss on both cheeks she was rewarded with a smile on Demi's face that had been missing until now. That happy countenance cemented the idea Nik planned to propose to Fran when the time was right.

She spoke to the baby. "Look who's here—your favorite uncles!"

He was witnessing another kind of miracle, one of communication despite the fact that Fran didn't understand Greek, nor did the baby comprehend English.

Nik and his brothers took turns kissing her, but the baby clung to Fran. The nurse came in with a bag of diapers and enough formula to satisfy the baby until they reached home. Fran changed her and put on the new pink outfit, then looked around. "Who wants to feed her?"

Sandro took Demi from her arms, but the baby wanted none of it. "Well, that settles it." He kissed her curls before returning her to Fran's arms. "I'm afraid you're stuck, *Kyria* Myers."

"Call me Fran, and I don't mind at all."

The nurse handed her a bottle. Soon Demi had settled down to drink, content for the moment. She eventually burped a couple of times, announcing she'd drained it. More chuckles ensued from everyone. Despite the sadness ahead when they returned to Mykonos, Demi was the bright light that kept them all from sinking right now.

Nik walked over to Fran. "We're ready to go. I'll carry Demi to the helicopter. After we're onboard the plane, we'll eat breakfast." He relieved her of the baby and wrapped her in the quilt.

"Come on, *Demitza*. We're going for a ride."

Fran followed him from the room with his brothers. Once they rode the elevator to the roof, they helped her into the helicopter while he climbed in with Demi. He handed her over to Cosimo who strapped her in the infant seat next to Fran. His brothers sat on the opposite side.

When everyone was settled in, Nik noticed Fran reach for Demi's little hand before he took his place in the copilot's seat. The gesture touched him and told him even more about the compassionate woman who'd put her vacation plans aside to make Demi secure. Again he wondered how many other women he'd known would have done that.

In a few minutes they lifted off and made a beeline for the airport. He heard his brothers talking to Fran. "We want to thank you again for all your help so far. Demi hasn't been around other people besides family, so it's a real surprise that she's taken to you."

"I'm sure it's because I was the one who found her in the garden. She'd been lying there helpless all night."

"I think it's more than that," Sandro confided. "You have a loving way with her like our sister."

"Well, thank you. It's been my pleasure to stay with her, believe me."

"How long will you be in Greece?"

"I fly home in less than two weeks."

Maybe not, Nik mused. Before he introduced Fran to his parents, he needed to have a private talk with her. The best place to do that would be aboard the jet in the compartment he used for his office.

"I guess you know our parents would like you to stay with us on Mykonos for part of the time."

"That's kind of them, Cosimo, but it's really up to

my friend Kellie Petralia who invited me here. She'd planned this time for us to be together."

"She and her husband are welcome to stay with us, too," Sandro chimed in.

"Your parents told me as much on the phone."

"That's because we're all grateful to you."

Grateful didn't exactly cover Fran's deepest feelings. She'd been empty for too long. To suddenly be taking care of a baby who was content to be in her arms made her feel whole for the first time in years. Even though she would have to relinquish Demi tomorrow, she would savor this sweet time with her today and tonight.

In her teens she'd been told she couldn't have children. It had been like a light going out, but over the years she'd come around to the idea of adoption.

During the short flight to Thessalonika, Fran looked out the helicopter window at the sparkling blue Aegean below, wishing she could concentrate on the spectacular panorama. Instead she found herself reliving the painful moment when Rob had shattered her dreams of being a mother.

Even if it were possible to love another man again, the idea of meeting one who said he'd be willing to adopt wasn't an option for her. Maybe one day she might meet and fall in love with a widower who had a child or children. At least then she could take over the mother role to help fill that empty space in her heart.

She simply couldn't see it happening, but Kellie wouldn't let her think that way. Dear Kellie... Her friend was in turmoil right now.

Her eyes strayed to Demi who was wide awake for the trip. She made sounds and was growing restless at being confined. In order to placate her, Fran got out another bottle of formula to keep her happy. Demi held it and mostly played with it, only sucking on the nipple without absorbing a lot of liquid. Her two bottom teeth had come in, helping her to tug on it.

Fran was amused to see the funny behavior coming from this child who could win the most beautiful baby of the year award. That was because she had the classic features of her mother and glossy black hair like Nik's... and his brothers, Fran hastened to remind herself.

But Nik possessed an unconscious sensuality and sophistication that stood out from his siblings. She put her head back for a minute and closed her eyes so she wouldn't keep staring at the back of his head where a few tendrils of black hair lay curled against his neck. Once in a while he turned to say something to his brothers and she glimpsed his striking male profile and chiseled jaw.

Dressed in the light brown sport shirt and dark trousers he'd changed into at the hotel last night, there was no man to match him. The celebrated bachelor's appeal went far beyond the physical. He was warm and generous. She doubted he had a selfish bone in his body. Nik was so different from Rob....

Before long the helicopter landed, and they were driven to the Angelis Corporation jet, the size of a 727, waiting on the tarmac. While Sandro and Cosimo helped her and Demi onboard, Nik excused himself to talk to the people who'd taken care of putting his family's bodies in the cargo area.

A few minutes later he walked down the aisle toward her. After speaking to his brothers on the way, he came to sit on the other side of her and Demi. His half smile turned her heart over.

"The flight to Mykonos won't take too long. Then it's just another short helicopter ride to the villa. After we reach cruising speed, we'll eat breakfast, then I'd like to have a private talk with you in the compartment behind the galley. My brothers will entertain Demi."

She nodded, but couldn't help but wonder what was on his mind. He'd said something about a position in front of the doctor. What exactly had he meant?

She strapped herself in, and the jet took off. Like clockwork, the minute the Fasten Seat Belt light went off, the steward started serving their food. Fran needed a good meal, if only to brace herself for their talk.

Once the steward removed their trays, she undid Demi long enough to change her diaper. Nik got up from his seat and reached for another bottle in the hospital diaper bag. Once Demi was strapped in again, he kissed her and gave her the bottle to keep her occupied.

Touching Fran's elbow he whispered, "Follow me."

She did his bidding, but it was but a few seconds before they could hear Demi cry. Fran felt like the biggest meanie on earth, but she kept going. Once inside the compartment set up as a den with a computer, Nik closed the door and invited her to sit in one of the club seats opposite him. They could still hear Demi's cries though they sounded fainter. Fran knew the baby's uncles would take care of her, but the sound of her distress tugged at her.

Nik sat back in his club chair with that unconscious aura of a CEO at home in his world. His dark eyes seemed to scrutinize her as if he were looking for secrets she might be hiding. Her pulse quickened in response.

"Before we reach Mykonos, I wonder if you'd answer some personal questions for me."

Personal? "If I can."

"Are you a full-time employee at the hospital?"

"Yes."

He cocked his head. "What would happen if you needed more time off? Would they give it to you without it causing you problems?"

"I think so, but it would have to be because of an emergency."

"Of course. One more question. Are you involved with another man right now?"

She blinked. He obviously had a reason for all this probing. "No."

"And your friend Kellie. Would it disappoint her terribly if you didn't spend your vacation with her?"

"Yes," Fran answered honestly. "Why?"

Her question caused him to lean forward with his hands clasped. His intelligent dark eyes fused with hers. "Because I have a great favor to ask of you. I know I don't have the right, but Demi's needs are going to be top priority for my family in the days ahead."

"I can understand that."

"Judging by her behavior around you in the hospital, and including the fact that she started crying the minute we walked away from her a few moments ago, it's clear Demi has formed a strong attachment to you. I dread what things are going to be like when you leave on your vacation with Kellie. She'll not only be looking for her parents, but for you. That's what's got me worried."

Fran had been worried about it, too, but she would

never have brought it up. "Surely when she's surrounded by your family again, she'll get through the transition."

He inhaled sharply. "I would have thought her seeing me and my brothers would have been all she needed. We're a close family and get together often. But this experience has traumatized her in some way we don't understand. If she isn't clinging to us, then I don't expect she'll want anyone else, not even the staff who are familiar to her."

"What about your parents? Your mother? Does she look like Melina?"

"They shared certain traits." His eyes stared into Fran's. "But I don't know if Demi would cling to them the way she does to you. I'm very interested to see what happens when she's with them again. Something tells me it won't be enough to make the baby feel secure."

"You'll have to give Demi time."

"That goes without saying. Nevertheless, I plan to consult a child psychiatrist after the funeral is over. Depending on what he or she says, I'll go from there. But for the time being, I'd like to hire you to take care of Demi until you have to get back to Philadelphia. By then I'll have some idea of how to proceed."

Fran stirred in the chair. While trembling with excitement at the prospect of loving that little girl for a while longer, she knew how painful it would be when she had to say a final goodbye. She'd known a lot of pain in her life. First the death of her brother, then the death of a dream that had ended in divorce. She might not have lost Rob in death, but it felt like one.

No brother, no husband, no child of her own after three years of marriage. Fran knew herself too well. Another twenty-four hours taking care of that precious baby would be hard enough. But ten more days? She couldn't risk the inevitable pain. It would come and she wouldn't be able to stop it.

"When she's been with your parents, or one of your brothers' families, she'll eventually adapt."

One black brow dipped. "I don't know. It's too soon to work all that out and I want a doctor's opinion first. The one thing I do know is that Demi wants *you*. If you could bring yourself to help us out here, you'll be handsomely compensated. Anything you want."

She shook her head. "That's very generous, Nik, but I wouldn't do it for the money."

He sat back again. "If Kellie doesn't mind a change in your plans, would you consider it? You'll stay in an apartment at the villa. There's a guest room and another smaller room we'll set up as a nursery. Kellie is welcome to be with you any time you want. But I guess I haven't asked the most important question. Is this something you wouldn't mind doing?"

Mind? If he had any idea... Demi had climbed into her heart where she would always stay. Discovering the baby in that garden was as if providence had set the baby down in those bushes at the precise moment for Fran to find her.

But the flags had gone up, warning her that if she told him she wouldn't mind at all, she could plan for rivers of anguish down the road when she had to tear herself away from that baby. It was a trauma she'd never get over.

"Fran?" he prodded. His smoky-sounding tone defeated her.

Although the youngest, Nik clearly carried the weight of the Angelis family on his shoulders. She had noticed how his brothers looked to him. This was a problem none of them had faced before. At the moment she recognized he needed a different kind of help and wanted Fran's.

But for her own self-preservation, she needed to remain firm. "It isn't a case of minding. It's just that I know what Kellie's answer will be when I ask her. We've been planning this trip for a long time. It will upset her too much and I can't disappoint her. I'm sorry. But until the funeral is over, I'll be happy to help out."

"Then I'm grateful for that much." He got to his feet. "Shall we get back to Demi before my frantic brothers come bursting in here with her?"

Fran had hated disappointing him, but her first priority had to be to herself.

CHAPTER FOUR

AT THREE THE NEXT afternoon, Nik left Fran holding the baby while he walked out to meet Leandros and his wife at the helicopter pad behind the villa. They'd been paying their respects to the other family, the ones who had lost their parents in the tornado and who couldn't get away before now.

"Fran will be relieved you're here now. It's all that matters." He led them out to the patio of the Angelis family villa where everyone had congregated to talk and eat. More tears ensued while Leandros and Kellie commiserated with his family.

Incredibly, the pain of losing Melina and Stavros was softened by the joy of having found Demi alive, a blessing no one had expected. Nik was heartened to see his family's spirits had lifted despite their loss.

"It's all over the news," Sandro spoke up. "Demi is known as the Miracle Baby. Did you know the hotel in Leminos has become famous overnight?"

"So has the hospital," Cosimo declared. "They even interviewed Demi's doctor on the noon news."

Though the whole family was eager to hold her, Demi clung to Fran just as Nik had suspected she would. The only time she didn't cry was when his parents held her.

But after a few minutes, Demi was looking for Fran and making sounds that indicated she didn't want to be with anyone else.

Nik knew his parents were hurt, but they hid it well. When they had issued her an invitation over the phone to be their guest for as long as she wanted, they had had no idea they would need her on hand to keep Demi happy. He smiled to himself. Though Fran had turned him down about staying on, she didn't know this story wasn't over yet.

His father eyed Fran who was holding Demi against her shoulder. The baby looked around chewing on her teething ring. "Tell us what you thought when you found her. We want details," he beseeched her.

Fran broke into a tender smile. Once more she repeated her amazing tale. "The hotel is situated on a corner of the street. My first thought was that her mother or father had been walking her in a stroller on the other side of the hotel when those gale-force winds drove Kellie and me to run inside for shelter.

"It seemed more than possible she'd been blown into the garden at the rear of the building. But if that were true, then where were her parents? I was in shock to think she'd been exposed to the elements all night. Honestly, she looked like she'd been dropped from the sky."

Nik's sisters-in-law made moaning sounds to think such a thing had happened.

Kellie sat forward. "I came around back and saw Fran holding a limp baby who was wearing only a torn shirt. I thought I was hallucinating."

"You weren't the only one," Fran added. "When neither the police or the hospital staff had heard of anyone looking for their baby, I began to think that's exactly what had happened, that she'd been carried by the wind and deposited in a cushion of bushes."

"But twelve miles—" Nik's mother cried out and put her hands to her mouth. "God wanted her to live." His father nodded his silver head and wept.

"Nik?" Fran eyed him from her place on the swing. "Has your family seen the pictures you took with your camera?"

He'd been planning to show them later. "Let's do it right now," he said, but he had difficulty talking because of the lump in his throat. After pulling out his phone, he clicked on to the picture gallery and handed it to his parents. "Slide your thumb across to see all of them. I took a few pictures in the hospital, too." He'd made certain he'd gotten some shots of Fran.

For the next little while his family and the Petralias took turns viewing them. Nik's six- and seven-year-old nephews were eager to look at them, too. The younger three- and four-year-olds had no idea what was going on and played with their toys. In the quiet, Fran's eyes met his. They were both remembering that surreal moment when she'd showed him the now-famous spot.

While everyone was talking, he walked over to her. "Do you think she's ready for something besides a bottle?"

"I hope so. She needs the nourishment."

"That's what I'm thinking. I'll tell cook to get out a jar of her favorite fruit and meat."

Fran hugged the baby. "You'd like some food, wouldn't you, sweetheart?"

Whether she wanted it or not, she needed it. Having made up his mind, Nik left the patio and headed for the kitchen. In a minute he returned with the food and the high chair that had been in use for several years.

He put it in front of Fran, then plucked the baby from her arms and set her inside it. The cook had given him a bib that he tied around her neck. Both Fran and Demi looked up at him in surprise.

Nik shot them an amused glance. "We'll both feed her," he explained and sat down on the swing next to her. "You take the turkey." He handed her the jar and a spoon. "I'll give her some plums."

"Coward," she whispered. Her chuckle filled him with warmth.

To his relief the baby began to eat, which meant her initial trauma had passed and she was relaxed enough to want her semi-solid food again. Once she'd been put in a private room at the hospital, the nurse hadn't been able to get her to eat anything. Fran had to see the transformation and think twice about turning him down when he asked her again.

"Well, look at you," she said to Demi with a big smile. "I didn't know you were such a good eater."

Demi beamed back at both of them. Nik had never actually fed Demi before. Aided and abetted by Fran, he found himself having more fun than he could remember. Some turkey clung to the baby's upper lip, making her look adorable. Both he and Fran chuckled in delight to see her behaving normally.

Soon she finished her food while the family looked on in varying degrees of interest and curiosity. They weren't used to seeing Nik feed her. But most of all, they were shocked at the way Demi responded to Fran. The hurt in his parents' eyes had intensified. It didn't surprise him when Nik's father eventually got up from his chair and walked over to give his granddaughter a kiss on the cheek.

"One would never know what you lived through, Demi," he spoke in Greek. "Come to your grandpa." He wiped her mouth with the bib, then untied it and picked her up to take her over to Nik's mother.

Demi adored her grandfather, but the further he took her from Fran, the more she squirmed and kept turning her head to find her. Nik's mother got to her feet and held out her hands to Demi, but the baby started to cry.

"What's wrong, darling?" his mother talked to her in their native tongue, attempting to cuddle her. "Tell me what's the matter."

Nik knew the answer to that. She wanted Fran. It really was astonishing to see that even with the entire family surrounding her, Demi wanted a stranger if she couldn't have her own mother and father. He eyed Fran covertly, daring her to close her mind and heart to what was going on here.

His stomach muscles tightened as he watched the looks of surprise and confusion from everyone, but especially at the pain on his parents' faces when Demi started crying in earnest.

They'd lost Melina, but it had never occurred to anyone that Demi wouldn't soak up the love they were ready to heap on her. Nik believed it was a passing phenomenon. It *had* to be. But right now something needed to be done to calm the baby down.

"You know what I think?" he said in English. "Demi's barely out of the hospital and needs to go to bed." So did his parents who needed to rest to get through this ordeal.

"Of course," his mother concurred.

"Fran and I will take her and put her down, then we'll be back."

He clutched the baby to him and started for the villa. Fran got up from the swing and followed him to the apartment. Earlier he'd asked the housekeeper to get it prepared. With the help of the staff, they'd moved the crib and other things from the nursery in Melina's apartment to the spare room. For now it would serve as a nursery while Fran took care of Demi.

Together they got the baby ready for her afternoon nap with a fresh diaper and a white sleeper with feet.

"You look so cute in this," Fran said, kissing her cheeks several times. Once again Nik marveled how natural she was with Demi, almost as if the baby were hers. Neither of them were bilingual, but it didn't matter. They spoke a special language of love that managed to transcend. Watching Demi, you'd think Fran was her mother. How could that be? Unless…

Was it possible that the baby's head had suffered an injury when she hit the earth and she'd developed *amnesia*?

Were there cases of such a thing happening to an infant? Amnesia might explain her connection to Fran. She'd been the first person Demi saw when she'd awakened in the hospital.

But if that were true, then why did she respond to the family, to Nik? Though it was half-hearted, she did recognize everyone. He was baffled and anxious to talk to a doctor first thing in the morning.

Nik drew a bottle of premixed formula from the bag. When Fran put the baby in the crib, he handed Demi her bottle. Speaking Greek to her, he told her he loved her and wanted her to go to sleep.

Before she started drinking, the baby made sounds and stared up at the two of them with those dark brown eyes that could have been Melina's.

"Come on, Fran," he whispered. "Let's go."

"See you later, sweetheart." Fran patted her cheek, then started to follow Nik out of the room. They'd no sooner reached the door than Demi burst into tears.

Fran looked at him with pleading eyes. "I can't leave her yet."

Nik had been counting on that. "She loves you."

Again Fran averted her eyes because she knew what he'd just said was true. "You go on and be with your family, Nik. I'm sure you have things to discuss before the funeral tomorrow. Tell Kellie to come and keep me company while Demi falls asleep."

"I will. Maybe when she sees how much the baby wants you, she'll tell you the vacation can wait a few more days."

"I—I don't think so." Her little stammer indicated she wasn't quite as confident as she'd been on the plane.

"We'll see," he murmured.

She gripped the bars of the crib. "The baby's worn-out from all the excitement, but still needs time to settle down and get sleepy. I'll join you on the patio later."

This extraordinary woman was right on all counts, but if the truth be told, Nik would rather stay in here with her. "All right, but I'll be back soon to relieve you if she proves too restless."

He strode swiftly through the villa to the patio and sought out Kellie. "Fran wants to talk to you. I'll show you to the nursery."

She spoke to Leandros who nodded his head, then she followed Nik through the house. Before they entered the apartment he said, "I'm not sure there wouldn't have been a catastrophe tonight if Fran weren't here to take charge of Demi."

Kellie smiled at him. "After college she went into hospital administration, but they soon found out she's a remarkable people person for the young and the old. That's why they put her in the position she holds now. I wager she's sorely missed already. I'm lucky she could take off these two weeks for our vacation."

Having seen her in action with Demi, Nik agreed. He also got the message from Kellie not to count on Fran's generosity beyond tonight. In fact, he was sure he'd been warned off, in the nicest way possible. While cogitating on that thought, he was more determined than ever to prevail on Fran to remain longer.

They reached the door to the apartment. "Come find the family after my niece has fallen asleep."

A half hour later Fran tiptoed out of the nursery with Kellie and they went into the bedroom. "I think she'll stay asleep now. Tell me what's happened with Leandros?"

"If anything, things are worse. But before we get into that, tell me what's going on with Nik."

"What do you mean?"

Kellie sat down on the side of the king-size bed. "He has you ensconced in this fabulous apartment with the baby in the adjoining room, almost like you're a permanent fixture."

"I told him I'd help out until after the funeral tomorrow."

"But he'd like it to be longer, right?"

Nothing got past Kellie. Fran nodded. "On the flight

to Mykonos, Nik asked me if I would stay on to tend Demi until she's comfortable with the family again. He hopes I'll remain here until I have to go back to Philadelphia. I told him no because you and I were on vacation."

"Are you hoping I won't hold you to it?"

She shook her head. "No, Kellie. I only told him that as an excuse. This has nothing to do with you or our trip. I need to leave tomorrow before I find myself wishing I could take her back home with me. If it were possible, I'd like to adopt her."

"Adopt an Angelis?"

"I know how outrageous that sounds. That's why I'm glad we're leaving tomorrow."

Looking haunted, Kellie got up from the bed. "I know how attached you are to the baby already and would love to say yes to him."

"Actually, I wouldn't."

"You must think I'm being difficult, but it's because I'm afraid to see you get hurt again. When I think what you went through with Rob…"

Fran sucked in her breath. "Believe me, I don't want that kind of pain again either. When I found Demi in that garden, I felt like I'd been handed a gift. I wanted her to be mine. But she isn't! If I stayed here ten more days, it would kill me to have to walk away from her, traumatizing her once again. I refuse to put myself or her in that position. I've had too many losses in my life."

"Oh, Fran—" Kellie gave her a commiserating hug.

She wiped her eyes. "I'm glad we're leaving after the funeral. I need to put this experience behind me and forget Demi exists. It has dredged up too many painful memories. I need to move on."

By now Kellie's eyes were wet. "That makes two of us. Leandros doesn't want me working in his office."

"He wouldn't even consider it?"

"No. He says he wants to be able to come home to me after a hard day's work, but the reason is crystal-clear. Though he hasn't come right out and said it, our love life has never been satisfactory to him.

"How could it have been with a bride who was in terrible pain the first time he made love to her? His marriage to Petra was nothing like ours. They were expecting a baby when—when—" She couldn't go on. "That's why I have to put some real distance between us. Karmela can supply him what's missing. Our marriage is over."

"I can't bear it, Kellie."

"It's for the best. Like you, I refuse to wallow in any more pain. As for the Angelis family, they need to hire a nanny as soon as tomorrow after the funeral and get her installed right away."

"Agreed. I know Demi will miss me, but she'll get over it. She'll *have* to. I made that clear to Nik."

"For your sake, I'm glad." They eyed each other for a long moment. "Even though I'm nursing a horrendous headache, what do you say we put on our best smiles and go out to the patio as if nothing in the world is wrong? After we've mingled for a while, I plan to have an early night."

"So do I. Demi will be needing another bottle before sleeping through the night."

They reached the door. "Leandros will cover for me until he's ready for bed. It's what he's good at. You might as well know we haven't slept together for the last month."

Fran understood her pain. She hadn't slept with Rob for the three months leading up to their separation. It had been the beginning of the end.

The day was winding down. Nik's mother and sisters-in-law spoke together while he talked with the men. But they all stopped long enough to admire the two American beauties who'd just stepped out onto the patio.

At the first sight of Fran, Nik felt an unwanted quickening in his body. The same thing had happened at the hospital when they'd been removing their masks and gowns. In a very short time she'd grown on him despite the pain he was in.

Most of the Greek women he'd known and dated were more chatty and conscious of themselves, famous for drama on occasion. His sisters-in-law were like that. Fiery at times—beautiful—and they knew it. Melina hadn't been quite so theatrical. That's probably why she'd appealed to the quietly spoken Stavros.

Fran was an entirely different kind of woman. She seemed comfortable in her attractive skin, reminding Nik of still waters that ran deep. Did her calm aura hide unknown fires within? He felt in his gut this woman could become of vital importance to him.

After some soul-searching, he recognized his motivation to keep Fran in Athens wasn't driven exclusively by Demi's best interests. Already he was trying to find a way to persuade her to stay on for his own personal reasons. But he feared that if he lowered the bars to let her inside his soul and she couldn't take what he would be forced to tell her, blackness would envelop his world. He faced a dilemma he'd never experienced before.

Should he run from what he feared most? Or did he

reach out for the one thing that might bring him the greatest joy?

On impulse he turned to the others. "If you'll excuse me, I need to talk to *Kyria* Myers."

By now Kellie had joined her husband, leaving Fran alone. He watched her wander to the wall at the edge of the patio and look out over the water. Her violet-blue eyes flicked to his when she saw him approach. "I can't imagine gazing out on this idyllic view every night of your life. All the stories about the Greek Islands are true. You live in a paradise, especially here on Mykonos."

"I agree there's no place on earth quite like it. On the weekends, I look forward to leaving the office in Athens and coming home. The temperature of the air and the sea turns us into water babies around here."

She smiled. "There's an American artist who has done some serigraphs of Mykonos. He's captured the white cubic style of a villa like your family's to perfection."

"I know the artist you mean. I'm fond of his artwork, too, particularly several of his Italian masterpieces."

"Aren't they wonderful?"

He nodded, enjoying their conversation, but was impatient to get down to business. "How long did it take Demi to finally fall asleep?"

"Um, maybe ten songs," she quipped. Her gentle laugh found its way beneath his skin.

"Let's go for a walk along the beach." He took off his shoes. "Be sure to remove your sandals. You can leave them here by mine."

"All right." Together they walked down the steps

to the sand. From there it was only a few yards to the water. "Oh. Lovely. It warms my toes."

Nik chuckled. "Twilight is my favorite time to swim. If you wait a while, the moon will come up. Then everything is magical."

"It already is."

They walked in companionable silence for a long time. Unlike most women he knew, she felt no need to fill it in with conversation. That was a quality he liked very much, except for tonight. At the moment he had the perverse wish she would speak her mind. Fran knew he was waiting to hear she'd changed her mind.

Taking the initiative, he said, "Are you and Kellie still intent on leaving tomorrow?"

She slowed to a stop. In the dying light, she looked straight at him. "Yes. Much as I'd like to help you out, I'm afraid I can't. But I'll have you know it has been my privilege to take care of Demi over the last few days. If it's your wish, I'll stay with her until the funeral services are over. Then I'll fly back to Athens with Kellie and Leandros."

His heart clapped to a stop. She'd turned him down flat. Over his years in business, he'd made a study of people to find out what made them tick. Before Kellie Petralia had spent time alone with her in the bedroom, he could have sworn Fran was considering his proposition. He rubbed the back of his neck. Leandros's wife had a definite agenda and Nik's appeal to Fran had gotten in the way.

Trying a different tack he said, "Could you possibly wait another day? With the funeral tomorrow, I won't be able to do anything about Demi's care until the next day.

What I'd like to do is interview some nannies for the position. It would be a big help if you were there, too.

"Your hospital work makes you somewhat of an expert in reading people. If we both come up with our own questions, I'm sure we'll be able to pick the right nanny for her."

"I'm sorry, Nik, but I promised Kellie we'd leave as soon as you all came back from the interment. Surely your own mother and sisters-in-law would be the perfect ones to help out?"

Disappointed by her noncapitulation, he bit down hard on his teeth. "They would if Demi would let them hold her. I'm afraid a hysterical baby could put off a potential nanny."

"If that's the case, then you need to keep looking for one who can handle the situation, no matter how difficult."

Damn if beneath that ultra-feminine exterior she didn't think like a man....

He felt a grudging respect for her, but this battle was far from over and he was determined to win. "What if I offered you the job of permanent nanny? It's what I'd been thinking about all along after I saw how you cared for her in the hospital. No one could have been more like a mother. That's why she responded to you."

"Thank you for the compliment, but I already have a career," she came back without blinking an eye. "As much as I love that little girl—and who wouldn't?—it's a job, and the last one I'd want."

Nik was dumbfounded. "Are you so enamored of your hospital work, you can't imagine yourself leaving it for a position that could pay you an income to set you up for life in surroundings like this?"

"Actually, I can't, and I don't want that kind of money."

Then she belonged to a dying breed.

"Let me ask you the same question, Nik. Do you love what you do to make a living?"

His eyes narrowed on her appealing features, particularly her generous mouth. "What does one have to do with the other?"

"I was just thinking of a way to solve your problem. In the hospital, you treated Demi like a father would. Maybe you ought to become her nanny and give your brothers more responsibility for running the Angelis Corporation. Your sister Melina and Stavros would look down from heaven and love you forever for making such a great sacrifice."

Fran didn't know he'd agreed to be Demi's guardian if anything happened to them. Her comment found his vulnerable spot and pierced the jugular. He could feel his blood pressure climbing.

"Then again," she said softly, "you could find a wife who would love Demi and make a beautiful home for the three of you. That would take care of every problem. Your parents must be worried sick you haven't settled down yet."

Adrenaline pushed his anger through the roof. "Now we come to the crunch. After reading the tabloids on the plane, is it possible you're offering to become my bride and bring an end to my wicked ways? Is that what this verbal exercise has all been about?"

Her gentle laughter rang out in the night air. "Heavens, no. You're no more wicked than the next man."

While he digested that surprising comment she said, "I've been through marriage once and have no desire to be locked in that unhappy prison again. I was only teasing you, Nik, but it was wrong of me to try to lighten your mood on the eve of the funeral. Forgive me for that. I can see why you're such a powerhouse in business. You make it impossible to say no."

"Yet you've just said no to me." The nerve at his temple throbbed. This woman was twisting him in knots.

She eyed him critically. "You've told me you value what I've learned from my hospital work. If that's true, then listen to me. Demi's going to be all right. I promise. For a while we know she'll grieve for her parents, but in time she'll respond to your loving family.

"They're wonderful and they're all here willing to do anything. Let them help. Don't take it all on by yourself or you'll burn out."

"What are you talking about?" he growled with impatience.

"I'm talking about *you*. Leandros sings your praises as the new brains and power behind the Angelis Corporation. But you can't be everything to everyone every minute of the day and night the way you've been doing since you heard about the tornado. You remind me of Atlas carrying the world on your shoulders."

Atlas?

"I've seen it happen in families once a patient goes home from the hospital. There's always one person like you who carries the whole load, whether because of a greater capacity to feel compassion or a stronger need to give service. Who knows all the reasons? But the point is, this develops into a habit, and you're too young for this to happen to you."

Without question Fran Myers was the most unique

individual he'd ever met. No woman had ever confounded him so much before.

He sucked in his breath. "Let's go back, shall we? On the way, I want to hear about the reason why your marriage failed you to the point that you no longer believe in it."

Slowly they retraced their footsteps. "In a couple of sentences, I can tell you why it didn't work. He was the live wire at his law firm trying to make it to the top. Furthermore, he didn't feel he had the time to be a family man. He was too consumed by his work."

"What vital ingredient have you left out?"

When Fran almost stumbled, he knew he'd hit a nerve. "I'm afraid we both fell out of love. It happens all the time to millions of people."

"But not to someone like you. If he didn't have an affair, then what's the real reason it failed?"

"I'd rather not discuss it."

"Since you pretty well laid me out to the bare bones a little while ago, how about some honesty from you in return?"

"I suppose that would only be fair." She tossed her head back, causing the dark blond mass of gleaming hair to resettle on her shoulders. "You could say that when he didn't live up to the bargain we'd made before we married, there was nothing to hold us together any longer."

"Then he lied to you."

"I wouldn't say it was a lie… More of a human failing. When faced with the reality of what he'd committed to while we were dating, he couldn't go through with it. I didn't blame him for it, but my disappointment was so profound, my heart shut down."

"I'm sorry. How long were you married?"

"Three years."

And no children.

He wanted to know more. "Was he your first love?"

"No. Over the years I met and dated several men I thought might be the one. I'm sure the same experiences have happened to you."

"It's true I've enjoyed my share of women and still do. All of them have traits I admire."

"But so far none of them has delivered the whole package. At least that's what the tabloids infer," she added in a playful tone. "It was the same for me until Rob came along. He had everything that appealed to me and I didn't hesitate when he asked me to marry him."

Nik's dark brows lifted. "And once you'd each said I do, the one essential element to make your marriage work wasn't there after all, and it drove you apart."

"Precisely."

She was good at maintaining her cool, but every so often when their arms or legs brushed while they were walking, he could feel her trembling because she was holding back critical information. Her friend Kellie could enlighten him, but he knew deep down that wasn't the route to go. He'd find Leandros.

As if thinking about him conjured him up, they discovered him taking a swim. Like Nik, he'd been born on an island in the Aegean and found the water the ideal place to wind down at the end of the day. But Nik had to admit surprise his wife hadn't joined him.

"Hey, Leandros—" Fran called to him. "Where's Kellie?"

When he saw them, Leandros swam to shore. After picking up a towel he walked toward them while he dried himself off. "She had a headache and went to bed."

"After the horror of the last few days, I'm not surprised," she said in a quiet tone. "I'm ready to turn in myself." She glanced at Nik. "Thank you for your hospitality and the privilege of taking care of Demi one more night. I'll see you and your family in the morning before the funeral. Goodnight."

She gave Leandros a hug before she started for the steps leading up to the patio. Once at the top, she waved to them before disappearing inside the villa.

"Would you mind leveling with me about something?"

Leandros's gaze switched to Nik. "Not at all."

"I asked Fran if she'd be willing to stay on for another week to help while our family tries to find the right nanny. Because she looked after Demi from the moment she found her, I thought she might be willing. But when I asked her this evening, she indicated she's planning to travel with your wife and can't change her plans."

A grimace broke out on his face. "My wife's mind is made up."

There was a lot Leandros wasn't saying, but it was none of Nik's business until his friend chose to tell him.

"Then that relieves my fear. I thought maybe she'd said no to me as an excuse because of something I may have said or done to offend her. In my attempt to compliment her for the way she took care of Demi by asking her to stay on for a while longer, I may have accomplished the opposite result.

"As you saw earlier, my little niece clings to her and is unhappy with anyone else. When I told Fran she'd be well paid for her sacrifice, I think she took it as the final insult, which was the last thing I meant to do."

Leandros shook his head. "Not Fran. She stayed with your niece at the hospital because she wanted to. I'm sure she would have agreed to help you if Kellie weren't so insistent on their taking this trip."

"Where are they going?"

"On a driving trip to see other parts of Greece and do some hiking."

"I see."

"Fran's first marriage didn't work and Kellie has worried about her ever since. Just between us, my wife is determined to find Fran a husband."

That was an interesting piece of news. "Does she have someone particular in mind?"

"I doubt it. I think she's hoping they'll meet some unattached American over here on holiday with the right credentials who will sweep Fran off her feet. In the meantime, rest assured Fran's decision has nothing to do with you or the baby. I happen to know she's as crazy about kids as Kellie is."

Finally Nik had his answer though he already had proof how much she loved children by her attachment to Demi.

He patted Leandros's shoulder. "Thanks for the talk. You've relieved my mind in more ways than you know. See you in the morning. If I haven't told you yet, my family and I are honored that you'll be here for us."

"It's the least I can do for a good friend," Leandros's voice grated. "I plan to attend the services for the other family this weekend."

But Leandros's wife wouldn't be with him. Something was wrong and it gave him an idea.

"Leandros? Before you go to bed, there's something else I'd like to talk to you about it if you don't mind. I've been trying to think of a way to reward Fran for all she's done and would like to run it by you."

"Go ahead. I'm not ready for bed yet."

CHAPTER FIVE

THE ANGELIS FAMILY lived on a private part of the island overlooking a brilliant blue sea. Fran found the dazzling white villa with the main patio as the focal point for the family to congregate, an architectural wonder. She could see why the Cyclades was the desired vacation spot in Greece, especially this portion of the renowned Kalo Livadi Beach where she'd walked with Nik last night.

Their conversation had created a tension that had still gripped her after she'd gone to bed, making her sleep fitful. She'd never been so outspoken in her life with anyone, but fear of being in pain again had driven her to say those things to him.

While some of the staff came out to get things ready for the meal to be served when the family got back, Fran's gaze lit on the beautiful child whom she'd put in the high chair to feed her a midafternoon snack. She'd placed Demi beneath the shade of the umbrella while Fran sat in the sun to soak up what she could. Pretty soon everyone would return. After that, she and Kellie would leave for Athens.

Out of deference to his family, she'd dressed more formally in a light blue summer suit and white high heeled sandals. Beneath the short-sleeved jacket she wore a white T-shirt. After applying her lipstick, she'd fastened her hair back with a tortoise shell clip. She often wore it this way to work.

Rob had said he preferred it back because it made her look more sophisticated. For him, the right look was everything. But Fran had chosen to wear it this way today because Demi liked to pull on it and she was strong.

"Do you know you're the best eater?" Though the seven-month-old couldn't possibly understand her, she smiled and opened her mouth for more peaches. "You like these better than plums, don't you. Two more bites and you're all finished." She moved the spoon around to bait her before putting it in her mouth. Demi laughed, encouraging Fran to do it again.

As the baby laughed harder, a shadow fell over her. It couldn't be a cloud. She turned her head in time to see a somber-faced Nik staring down at her from those dark eyes she couldn't read. Standing there so tall and hard-muscled, he looked incredibly handsome in the midnight-blue mourning suit and tie he'd worn to the funeral.

"There's nothing like Demi's laughter to dissolve the gloom, is there?" he murmured before bending down to kiss his niece on both cheeks. "Sorry we're late, but there was a huge crowd at the burial and many people who wanted to express their sympathy."

Fran nodded, feeling his pain. Demi's parents had been laid to rest. She would never know them. The enormity of raising this little girl who would need the Angelis family from here on out settled on Fran like a mantle.

She could only imagine Nik's feelings of love mixed with inadequacy right now. Their whole family had to be weighted by the new responsibility thrust upon them. Moved with compassion, Fran got to her feet and wiped Demi's mouth with her bib. Driven by her own heart-felt emotions, she picked up the baby and handed her to Nik, who must be feeling empty inside.

"Demi's going to need all of you now. If you'll excuse me, I have to go finish the last of my packing."

She practically ran inside the villa so she wouldn't hear the baby start to cry. Nik was a big boy now. He would deal with this crisis in the expert way he handled all of his business transactions.

Fran had done her packing early, but she'd needed the excuse to tear herself away from Demi. To be sure she hadn't left anything behind, she made one more trip into the bathroom.

"Fran? Are you about ready?"

"Whenever you are." She came back out to find Kellie who'd changed from her black dress to white pleated pants and a watermelon-colored top.

"I asked Leandros to tell the family the three of us couldn't stay to eat. We've already said our goodbyes to them. I'll help carry your cases out to the helicopter pad." She took the big one while Fran reached for the smaller bag.

Halfway down the hall they met Leandros, whose drawn features aged him. He gave Fran a hug. "You look beautiful."

"Thank you," she whispered.

There was an ominous quiet as he took the suitcase from Kellie and they walked through the villa to the rear entrance. Neither of them had another word to say. Fran was so uncomfortable, she could scream.

When they stepped into the sunlight, Fran could see

the helicopter waiting for them in the distance. She almost ran toward it, but as she drew closer, she saw a tall figure talking to the pilot. It was Nik!

Her heart missed a beat because she'd thought she'd seen the last of him. When she'd handed Demi to him on the patio, she'd intended that to be her own form of goodbye.

"Here. Let me take your bag while you climb inside."

Fran had no choice but to give it to Nik before he helped her up. The touch of his hand sent fire through her body. No sooner had she found a seat than he joined her in the one next to her. Behind him came Kellie. Apparently their luggage had been put onboard ahead of time. Then Leandros climbed in next to the pilot and shut the door.

She turned to Nik in shock. "You're not staying with your family?" But her question came too late because the rotors whirred and they lifted off.

He gave her a ghost of a smile. "Last night after I went to bed, I thought about our conversation and decided to take your advice. Everyone who loves Demi is there to take care of her. I'm going to let them, and give myself a vacation. In another week they'll have sorted out what's best for her without my taking charge."

Guilt smote her for having been so outspoken. "You're joking...aren't you?" she blurted in consternation.

"Not at all. You made perfect sense. I'm afraid I have a tendency to do everything myself. Thanks to you, that's a flaw I'm going to work on. A vacation from my problems is exactly what I need. I haven't had a real one in over a year."

She blinked. "Where will you go?"

"Well, I was hoping you'd let me and Leandros drive you and Kellie around. I talked to him about it last night. I never drive anywhere anymore. Believe it or not, driving used to be one of my great passions. Not only would it be a great pleasure, but it would make me feel like I'd paid all of you back for everything you did for Demi and my family."

Kellie looked even paler than she had earlier in the morning. She shot Fran a private message before she looked at Nik. "That's very thoughtful of you, but Fran and I have decided to fly back to the States in the morning and vacation in California."

Uh-oh. For Kellie to have made a decision like that, the situation between her and her husband had reached flashpoint.

Nik's piercing gaze shot to Fran. "I haven't been there in years. How would you feel about having a third party along?"

Fran had no choice but to back up her friend. "I had no idea you could be such a joker."

"It turns out we make a good pair." His comment was meant to remind her of the way she'd talked to him last night. "But if you're not going to take me seriously, at least agree to have dinner with me this evening. I refuse to let you leave the country without enjoying a night out in the Plaka. I owe you a great deal for all you've done."

Afraid he would be unstoppable until she gave in, she decided to capitulate to that extent. "Your invitation sounds delightful, but if I say yes, it will have to be an early night."

"Good. In that case I'll ask Leandros to drop us off at my apartment. You can change clothes there. We'll go casual and play tourist while we walk around and eat what we want."

In the next instant he spoke to Leandros who nodded and gave instructions to the pilot. Soon Fran saw the glory of Athens spread before them in the late afternoon sun. The magnificent Parthenon, one of the most famous landmarks in the world, sat atop the Acropolis.

Seeing this sight from the air with Nik gave it special meaning. Just when she thought she'd figured him out, he did something unexpected that illuminated other appealing facets of his intriguing personality. She had to admit she wanted to spend the rest of the day and evening with him.

Right now his spontaneity thrilled her down to her toenails. With Rob every move had been calculated and planned out. She didn't want to compare the two men, but she couldn't help it. Rob wasn't unkind, but he'd expected her to conform. When she didn't, he went into a private sulk until she ended up being the one to apologize.

Nik, on the other hand, wouldn't know how to pout. He had hidden depths. Already she'd learned that his way was to zoom in and change the game plan if necessary to achieve the desired outcome. If he ever settled down, it would have to be with a woman who was even more unpredictable than himself. His psyche required a challenge.

Unfortunately Nik occupied too many of her thoughts and was becoming important to her. Any woman who became involved with him would know joy for a time, but in the end she'd pay for it. Wasn't that what Kellie had been saying about Leandros? The thought was terrifying.

Her mind was still full of him when the helicopter set
down on the helipad atop his apartment building. She
had to look away so she wouldn't get dizzy. This form
of transportation was as natural as breathing to busi-
nessmen like him and Leandros, but for Fran it would
have to become an acquired taste.

She turned to Kellie. Close to her ear she said, "I'll
see you later tonight."

"Be back before the clock strikes twelve," her friend
responded without mirth. Something dark was on Kellie's mind, leaving Fran troubled.

"I promise."

Nik grabbed Fran's bags. As they started for the stairs,
the helicopter lifted off, creating wind that molded her
skirt to her shapely legs. She caught at it with her hands,
but she was too late. When they entered the elevator,
he could see the flush that had crept into her cheeks.
How nice to be with a truly modest woman. It made
her more enticing to him.

"Here we are." The doors opened on his glassed-in
penthouse.

She stepped into the entrance hall. For a full minute
she appraised his fully modern apartment. "If I didn't
know better, I'd think I was in the control tower at the
airport."

He burst into laughter. Fran Myers was a breath of
fresh air. "I pretend Athens is the sea I miss when I'm
working in the city."

"The view is spectacular." She darted him a mischie-
vous glance. "I'd say Atlas has it pretty good splitting
his time between here and Mykonos."

"There's no Atlas here today. Haven't you noticed I'm not carrying the world on my shoulders?"

She studied him rather intently. "How does it feel to have all that weight removed for a little while?"

"I'll let you know later. First I'm sure you'd like to freshen up and change. The guest bedroom is down this hall." He set her bags inside the room. "Come into the living room when you're ready."

After closing the door, he walked to his bedroom for a shower. The idea of mingling with the crowds like any foreigner visiting Athens appealed to him. In deference to the heat, he changed into a well-worn pair of jeans and a linen sport shirt. Once he'd slipped on his sandals, he was ready to go.

The funeral had robbed him of an appetite, but the thought of being with Fran for the rest of the evening had brought it back. In fact, he was starving, and he wagered she was hungry, too.

More pleasant surprises greeted him to discover she was waiting for him at the window overlooking Stygmata Square. She'd put on a pair of jeans and a short-sleeved cotton top in a raspberry color. Her skin absorbed some of its hue. With her luscious honey-blond hair worn up, she presented a prim, cool look, making him long to put his lips to the curve of her neck.

He wandered over to her, once again aware of her wildflower fragrance. "We'll be walking in that area beyond the square," he pointed out. "I know a taverna that serves flaming sausages and grilled trout to die for. But if that doesn't appeal, there are dozens of restaurants offering what you would consider traditional Greek cooking."

Purplish-blue sparks lit up her eyes. "I'm one tourist who doesn't want traditional fare."

"Then be prepared for a gastronomical adventure. Let's go."

They rode the elevator and set off for the Plaka, the oldest part of the city. The place swarmed with visitors buying everything from furniture to jewelry in the shops lining the streets.

Hunger drove them to eat before they did anything else. She ate the trout and sausage right along with him. While they sat watching people and making up outrageous stories about who they were and where they'd come from, a girl selling flowers came up to their table.

"Isn't she sweet, Nik?"

"I agree." He bought a gardenia and put it in Fran's hair. The flower gave him an excuse to touch her. He wanted to touch her and the desire was growing.

Filled with good food and wine, he ushered her through the streets so they were constantly brushing against each other. While she marveled over all the souvenir shops, he marveled over her. She didn't want to buy anything, just look.

They ended up on top of the roof at the outdoor theater. With the Acropolis lit up in the background, they watched a local film with English subtitles. "The tragic story was ridiculous, but I loved it," she confided after they left to explore another street. Nik had been so aware of her, he hadn't been able to concentrate on the story line.

"Around the next corner is a taverna famous for its ouzo. Would you like to try some?"

"I experimented the last time I was in Athens and didn't care for it, but please don't let that stop you."

He smiled. "I don't like it either."

His comment prompted laughter from her. "How un-patriotic! I promise I won't tell anyone. Let's go down this narrow little alley and see what goodies could be hiding there."

Nik guided her along, amused at the way she ex-pressed herself.

One of the shops sold every type of cheap figurine, both religious and mythological. He thought she'd just look and keep going. Suddenly she stopped and picked up a small metal figure of Atlas holding up the world. She asked the owner how much. He named a price and she paid for it with euros.

"Shall I wrap it?"

"No. I'd like to take it just as it is."

When they'd walked a little ways further, she turned to Nik. "It's getting late and I have to go to Kellie's. Be-fore we leave, please accept this as my gift for show-ing me your world today. If you dare to keep it on your office desk, it will remind you about the necessity of taking a breather once in a while."

"The table by my bed will be an even better place for it," he fired back. "Each night it will be the last thing I see before I fall asleep. What greater way to help me keep my priorities in order."

They eyed each other for a moment. "Thank you for tonight, Nik. I've never had a better time."

Neither had he. The realization had made a differ-ent man of him.

He reached for the simple gift. It meant more to him than she could imagine. Instead of her begging him to buy her something the way one of his girlfriends would have done, she'd turned the tables. Her generosity of spirit ranged from saving a baby in the aftermath of a tornado, to presenting him a keepsake he'd always treasure.

"On our way back to the apartment, there's one more place you have to visit."

"Will I like it?"

"I'll let you be the judge."

Nik had been saving this stop until the end. He needed to get closer to her. The Psara taverna was housed in two old mansions with a roof garden. You could dance while you enjoyed a view of the Plaka. Getting her in his arms had been all he could think about.

He asked her to keep the figurine in her purse until later. After they'd consumed an ice cream dessert, he led her out on the floor. The band played the kind of rock whose appeal was fairly universal. At last he was able to clasp her to him while they moved to the music.

"You're a terrific dancer," he whispered against the side of her neck. "I could stay like this all night."

"I'm enjoying it, too."

"Have you dated much since your divorce?"

"There've been a few men, but if you're fishing for compliments, I can tell you now they don't dance like you."

"It's my Greek blood, but please continue. Flattery will get you everywhere, *Kyria* Myers."

Her body shook with silent laughter.

He relished the feel of her, pulling her even closer. "Don't fly back to the States tomorrow."

"I have to, Nik."

He pressed a kiss to her temple. "You do realize Kellie is running away from her husband."

The second he spoke, she stopped dancing and looked

up at him. "Did Leandros confide in you?" She sounded anxious.

"He's told me nothing, but it's clear they're having problems. I felt something was wrong from the start. Leandros isn't the same man I've known in the past."

"Neither is Kellie," she said in a tremulous voice.

Unfortunately it was Nik's fault the mood had been altered. "It's eleven-thirty. I heard her warn you not to be late. Let's go back for your cases. My driver will run us to their apartment. Are your bags packed?"

"Yes. I put them outside the bedroom door."

"Then I'll have them brought down."

As they moved through the crowds, he pulled out his phone to make the arrangements. When they reached his apartment building, the limo was waiting for them. He helped her in the back. Once he'd told his driver where to take them, he got in across from her so he could look at her. She had a glow about her he'd noticed while they were dancing.

"You're not really going to California."

She put the flat of her hands against the seat. "I don't honestly know."

"So if I flew over to the States, too, would I find you home tomorrow evening, or not?"

"Are you pursuing me?" she asked with refreshing bluntness.

"Isn't that obvious? I know you're not indifferent to me."

She stirred in place. "No woman could be indifferent to you, Nik, and you know it."

"So you're already branding me as a Romeo with no staying power."

Fran looked away. "You said it, I didn't."

"The tabloids never print the truth, but the public will consume it."

She rolled her eyes. "Give me a little credit for not believing everything I read. As long as you're still single, I guess it's your lot to be labeled. But I haven't done that."

"If this isn't about me, then it's personal where *you're* concerned."

"Not at all. But we both know you won't be making any trips to Pennsylvania."

"If you knew the real me, you wouldn't make such a careless statement."

In the silence that followed, her cell phone rang. He checked his watch. "It's five to twelve, Cinderella."

She eyed him almost guiltily before pulling it from her purse to check the caller ID. "It's Leandros—" Her voice sounded shaky before she clicked on. Once she'd said hello, the color drained out of her face. She only said a few more words before hanging up.

"What's happened?"

"It's Kellie. This evening at the apartment she became ill and fainted. They're in the E.R. at the Athens regional medical center. Will you please ask your driver to take us there?"

Nik alerted him, then moved across to sit next to her. Without conscious thought he drew her into his arms. Whispering into her hair he said, "I'm sure whatever it is, she's going to be all right."

If Nik just hadn't joined her on the seat…

If he hadn't held her like some cherished possession…

While they'd been dancing earlier, the contact had been wildly disturbing. But this comforting tenderness was too unexpected and welcome for her to move away from him. She'd been worried sick about Kellie. Now her worst fears were confirmed and he knew it.

"Do you have any idea what could have brought on her fainting spell?" His lips grazed the side of her forehead before she buried her face in her hands.

"You might as well know the truth. She's going to file for a legal separation after she's back in Philadelphia. They probably quarreled tonight. Kellie's emotions have been so fragile, I was afraid the stress might be too much."

"I didn't realize their problems had reached such a serious state. Otherwise I wouldn't have suggested the four of us take a trip together."

His sincerity reached her. "Don't feel guilty. In truth, I didn't suspect anything was wrong until she called me several weeks ago and insisted I take my two-week vacation right now. She said Leandros would be away on business and it would be the perfect time.

"They've been so happy, I couldn't believe she didn't want to travel with him the way she always does. That was my first warning all wasn't well."

"I'm sorry for them—and you." The limo pulled up near the doors of the E.R. "Let's find Leandros."

To Fran it was déjà vu as they entered the emergency room. Nik must have been having similar thoughts because his hand tightened on her arm. "Hard to believe it was only a few days ago I was rushing into the hospital to find out if the baby you'd rescued was our little Demi."

"Thank heaven it was!"

An ashen-faced Leandros came forward and put an arm around her. "Thanks for coming."

"As if I wouldn't. Do you know why she fainted?"

"The doctor couldn't find anything wrong, but he's still waiting for the blood-test results. Kellie doesn't want me in there and is asking to see you. Maybe if you talk to her, she'll settle down."

She'd never seen Leandros this frantic. "I'll go to her now. Where is she?"

"In the last cubicle."

"Try not to worry." She turned to Nik. "I'll be back out in a few minutes."

His compassion-filled eyes played over her features. "Take as long as she needs. I'll keep Leandros company."

"Thank you." She had an urge to kiss his cheek for being so understanding, but she held back. Without a minute to lose, she hurried through the E.R. and pulled the blue curtain aside.

"*Fran*—I thought you'd never get here."

"I'm so sorry, Kellie." She pulled up a chair. "How are you feeling right now?"

"Foolish. The doctor just came in and said nothing showed up on the tests. He says I fainted because I hadn't eaten all day. They gave me something to eat so I'm fine now. I'd like to get out of here and check into a hotel. The last thing I want is to go home with Leandros."

"He won't allow you to go anywhere without him. At least not tonight. Kellie? What else aren't you telling me? This is truth time. I can't do anything to help you if I don't know what's going on."

She sat up. "Not ten minutes after we arrived back, Karmela let herself in the apartment carrying a stack of work for Leandros to look over. She looked positively shocked to find me there."

Fran's eyebrows knitted together. "If she had plans to be alone with him, *she* should have been the one who fainted to realize you weren't on vacation with me yet."

"She's not the type to faint. That woman is as cool as the proverbial cucumber, treating me like I was the interloper and not his wife. No doubt she was allowed to use the security hand code to get in while her sister was alive and Leandros never deleted it.

"Leandros disappeared into the study with her for a few minutes. When she came out again, she flashed me this satisfied smile and bade me a safe flight in the morning. Fran—how could she have known my plans if Leandros hadn't discussed them with her? I don't want her knowing my business. I tell you, that was the last straw."

She groaned. "It would have been for me, too."

"When he came to find me, I was in the kitchen getting some juice and didn't say anything to him about her. He hovered around me until it drove me positively crazy, so I said goodnight and went to bed in the guest bedroom. It wasn't long before he came in and found me on the phone with Aunt Sybil. He told me to hang up because he wanted to have a serious talk with me."

"Did you?"

"Yes. I've never seen him in a rage before. He swore he didn't know Karmela would be by. The more he tried to explain his way out of it, the more I couldn't listen to him. Suddenly I felt so sick I passed out."

"I'm not surprised. Under the circumstances it's a good thing we're flying home tomorrow."

"Please forgive me, Fran. I'm ashamed to have to

confess I got you to Athens on my terms, not yours. It was horribly selfish of me when you wanted to wait until September."

"None of that matters. You need help."

"So do you," came Kellie's cryptic comment. She stared hard at Fran. "You're back late. I don't need to ask if you had a good time with Nik tonight."

"I did." It was a night she'd always remember.

"With that droopy gardenia in your hair, I can just imagine. Did he put it there before or after he kissed you?"

"There was no kiss." Except on her forehead.

"Not yet maybe, but it's coming. It's the Angelis charm working like clockwork. Just be careful you don't get completely sucked in."

"Why do you say that?"

"He already wants to go on vacation with you!"

"Kellie—he was only flirting."

"No. Nik Angelis is a compelling force in the corporate world, and he's an even more compelling sensual force when it comes to women. One of the secretaries in Leandros's office says he's had a string of them over the years. Leandros claims that when Nik wants something, he's relentless until he gets it. I can see where his persuasion tactics are leading where you're concerned."

"In what way?"

"He wouldn't think twice about asking you to quit your job at the hospital and move to Greece in order to become his niece's nanny."

Fran swallowed hard. "He already has. I turned him down. When the doctor at the hospital in Leminos mentioned he'd like to hire someone like me, Nik said something about having other plans in mind for me."

"I knew it!" Kellie muttered. "He's going to use every trick in the book to get you to take care of Demi. His plan is to make the moves on *you* to ensure victory. He's counting on a beautiful, vulnerable divorcée like you to cave. Have you told him you can't have children?"

"No, of course not."

"Then don't! That piece of information would be all he needed to get you to say yes. You can't do it, Fran, or you'll be facing even greater heartache than with Rob. He's got enough money to buy anyone he wants, but not you—" Her eyes pooled with moisture. "I say this because you're the best person I've ever known and you're *beyond* price."

"Oh, Kellie—" She gave her friend a long, hard hug.

"Promise me you won't let him get to you. If you do, it will mean you've given up on marriage altogether. You and I have talked about you falling in love again with a widower who has small children. Isn't that what you said?"

She pulled away from Kellie and wiped her eyes. "Yes, and you know it's what I'd like to happen."

"Then if you really mean that, don't get any more involved with Nik. I promise that if you do, you'll end up being stuck in the Angelis household as nothing more than a glorified servant. I don't care how strong your maternal feelings are for Demi. The years pass quickly. Think, Fran! One day she'll grow up and won't need you anymore. *Then* what will you do? You'll be too old for what you really want, and you'll live the rest of your life with a broken heart! After we're home I'll concentrate on helping you meet a terrific guy. There are hundreds of widowers looking for a wife online through a dating service."

"Ugh. That sounds horrible."

"Maybe not. You deserve to meet someone fantastic and fall in love with him. It happens to lucky couples all the time. Second marriages can be wonderful if you're not desperate, and if you take the time to meet that one person you can't live without."

"I know."

"Then remember something else. One of these days Nik's parents will bring pressure to bear and he'll have to get married, thus joining the ranks of his married brothers. They'll all have families except for you. So, what then? When Demi goes to college, will you go back to the States and get another job at another hospital, only to keep taking care of other people?"

The words stung, but she knew Kellie was saying them partly from her own pain and partly to help Fran think straight.

"You need to take charge of your life and live for *you*. I think you should have gotten out of your marriage the first time Rob said he didn't want to adopt. That was a year into your marriage. Look at the time you've wasted! I never said anything to you about it, but I wanted to."

Fran eyed her friend in surprise. "I had no idea you felt this strongly about it."

She bit her lip. "You don't know half of the things I thought about Rob and his utter selfishness where you were concerned. Your situation has made me take stock of my marriage. That's why I'm planning to separate from Leandros. I refuse to hang around another year or two while he and Karmela are involved. I don't know if they're actual pillow friends yet, but don't think she isn't lying in wait for the opportunity.

"On our drive back to Athens yesterday, it was like talking to a wall. He's in denial over her infatuation with him, but all the signs are there. After he tires of her, he'll want someone else yet expect me to look the other way. I knew it was too good to be true that he fell in love with me, but idiot that I am, I was so crazy about him, I left the blinders on."

She grabbed Fran's arms. "Don't do what I did— don't be charmed by Nik and his Greek-god looks. Don't let him get to you. Above all, don't sleep with him. He can pour it on like Leandros. It's their gift and their curse."

"*Kellie*—I've never seen you like this before."

"That's because I realize my marriage was a mistake. Karmela was in the picture from the first time I met Leandros. The warning signs were there, but I didn't pay any heed to them."

Fran was shaken because, despite her friend's bitterness, she was making sense.

"When I get back home, I'm filing for a divorce through my uncle's attorney. I'll stay with them until I figure out what I'm going to do."

"Do they know your marriage is in trouble?"

"Not yet."

Fran folded her arms against her waist. She threw her head back. "Out of all the marriages I've seen, I thought yours was the most solid. I have to tell you I'm devastated over this."

"I've been in agony since I realized Karmela was never going to go away. So don't let Nik talk you into something that will be difficult for you to get out of.

No matter how much that little girl tugs at your heart, she's not yours! She belongs to the Angelis family. They circle their own and you won't be an integral part of anything."

Fran shot to her feet, not needing to hear any more. "Do you want me to come back to the apartment to-night?"

"No. That would be the last straw for Leandros. I need to show him I'm in control and can handle life on my own. He thinks I'm a pushover. Well, no lon-ger! He should have married Karmela. I can't imagine why he didn't."

She let out an anguished cry. "Tell Nik to drive you to the Cassandra. I've already made arrangements for you to stay there in our private suite. We'll pick you up in the morning on our way to the airport."

"I'll be ready." She leaned down to give her a hug. Her eyes misted over. "You have to know my heart's breaking for you and Leandros."

"Now you have some idea of how I felt when you told me Rob didn't want to adopt after all. But you got through that terrible ordeal. Given time, I will, too."

Fran blew her friend a kiss, then slipped past the curtain and headed for the E.R. lounge. Both men got up when they saw her. Leandros's grave countenance haunted her. "How is she?"

"She's surprisingly good and ready for us to fly home in the morning. I'll watch out for her, Leandros. I'm so sorry this has happened. Obviously she needs her space. Once back in Philadelphia, time will have a way of making her see things more clearly. One thing I do know. She loves you with every fiber of her being. Don't ever forget that." Her voice shook.

His lips tightened. "I've forgotten nothing," he rapped out. "If she still wants to fly home in the morning, I'll fly her there in my jet. We have things to discuss. As you know, we've made arrangements for you to stay at the Cassandra tonight. Tomorrow morning my driver will be there to take you to the airport. I've booked you first class on a flight leaving at eight."

CHAPTER SIX

THIS WAS LEANDROS at his most intimidating. The situation was out of Fran's hands. She gave him a last kiss on the cheek. Nik grasped her elbow and led them out to the limo where he sat next to her.

"You're staying with me tonight. It's late, and it would be absurd for you to go anywhere else when I have a perfectly good apartment going to waste. Tomorrow will be a new day. After a solid night's sleep you can make decisions. Who knows, you might even decide to finish your vacation here."

The fight seemed to have gone out of her. "You've talked me into it. Thank you," she half sighed the words. "I'm drained, as I'm sure you are. I can't tell you how much I appreciate your generosity."

He flashed her a white smile that melted her bones. "At last I can do something for you."

"How many times do I have to remind you that taking care of Demi was a joy?" All of a sudden her voice caught. "Have you had any word from your family yet?"

"Yes. My father called."

"They must miss you terribly."

"I didn't get that impression. He phoned to thank me for bringing Demi home to them. He said my mother is a different person now that she has the baby to worry about. Demi fussed and cried all day, but the girls helped her and by bedtime she'd calmed down."

"I miss her, Nik."

"She's never off my mind either. My father says having Demi there has chased away the darkness and spirits are improving. He also admitted he envies me for being able to look forward to work. I told him he retired too soon and should come back in the office for half days, or at least for several times a week."

Nik was a wonderful son. Though Kellie had spoken the truth about Nik's determined nature, there was a noble side to him she couldn't dismiss. "That must have thrilled him."

"He said he'd think about it, which tells me he wants to keep his hand in things. I told him something else."

"What was that?"

"I've gone on vacation for a week and have left all the worry to my assistants. I suggested to Father he might want to check up on things while I'm gone."

"And?" she prodded because his eyes were smiling.

"He didn't say no."

"If he's anything like you, I bet he can't wait to dig back in."

"I'm sure you're right. So you see, taking your advice is already paying dividends. If you hadn't convinced me to let go, I wouldn't have realized my father is still struggling with his retirement. I owe a great deal of what's going on at the villa to you, Fran."

Before she could think, he pressed a light kiss to her lips. It only lasted for a breathless moment, but the aftershocks traveling through her nervous system were as powerful as Kellie's warning. *Don't do what I did—*

*don't be charmed by Nik and his Greek-god looks. Don't
let him get to you.*

He grasped her hand. "Speaking of vacations, you
could use a break from worry about Kellie. Left alone
with Leandros who plans to stay in Philadelphia with
her for a while, she'll have time to consider everything
and rethink her decision to leave him. Why don't you
stay on in Greece for a few more days? If you're not
there then Kellie and Leandros will be forced to con-
front their feelings. I know that Leandros won't want
a divorce."

That sounded encouraging. Maybe Kellie had gotten through to him after all....

"To my knowledge, there's no finer man. I get the
impression Kellie is his whole world."

"She worships the ground he walks on, too. I liked
him the first time I met him and that has never changed.
But I'm not married to him. Their personal problems
are none of my business."

Except Fran knew what was tearing her friend apart.
It wasn't just about Karmela. Sometimes Fran got the
feeling Kellie was using Karmela as an excuse to cover
her own insecurities. She'd married a powerful man
whose first marriage had been happy. Kellie needed to
talk to someone professional about her problems.

"In that case, let's concentrate on enjoying our vacation," Nik suggested.

Fran chuckled to cover the sudden spike of her pulse.
"*Our* vacation? I didn't know we were going on one."

"Leandros wants time alone with his wife and you're
still here in Greece, ostensibly to travel. Does the
thought of hanging out together frighten you?"

A small tremor rocked her body.

"I'll ask you again. Are you afraid at the thought of being alone with me?"

Adrenaline spilled into her veins. "Why would I be?"

"Liar," he whispered.

His response made her laugh before she removed her hand.

"Admit you're afraid you'll like it too much."

He knew her too well. "Oh, I can admit to that already. It's what happens when the vacation is over that bothers me."

"Forget about the over part. When you're on vacation, you're not entitled to think, only to accept everything that comes as a special gift."

Her lips curved. "Your spin on the subject is without equal."

"I take it you can't wait for us to embark on our journey. Where would you like to go?"

"That's easy. How about a hike to the top of Mount Olympus?" she teased.

"The home of the gods."

"It's so famous, I want to climb it. Though I might be out of shape, Kellie and I planned to do it before a tornado swept through Greece and changed all our lives." She hated the throb in her voice.

"I can't think of anything I'd like more. We'll not only hike, we'll camp out. It's my favorite thing to do besides water sports."

"And driving," she added.

He grinned. "Your mind is a steel trap. This trip will be an experience to remember. I'll throw all my camping gear in the helicopter and we'll take off for Pironia tomorrow after breakfast. That's the start of the trailhead."

"You've climbed it, of course."

"Twice. Once with my brothers and another time with my friends."

She darted him a glance. "Is there anything you haven't done?"

"I haven't climbed all our Greek mountains yet, and I've never gone camping with a woman."

"That's probably the best idea you've ever had."

Once again he broke into the kind of deep masculine belly laughter that shook the back of the limo and warmed her insides, neutralizing Kellie's concerns for her for the moment.

Nik drew Fran to the side of the forest trail to allow a team of donkeys carrying packs to the refuge to go on ahead of them. This was a good place to stop for a drink of water. They'd been hiking for over an hour, passing and being passed by other hikers.

In another hour they would reach the refuge where everyone would spend the night. Nik had another place in mind where he would set up camp for them in total privacy. Tomorrow they'd climb to the top of Mytikas, the highest peak.

He hadn't known what to expect, but so far Fran had kept up with him, carrying her own backpack without complaint. She'd worn her hair up again to keep it out of her face. In jeans and a layered cream-colored top that her figure did amazing things for, he was hard-pressed to look at anything else.

"Are you ready to move on? We'll ascend a gorge and then you'll see the red top of the refuge."

"How high up is it?"

"Two thousand meters."

"Are we going to stay there tonight?"

"No. We'll set up our own camp above it. You don't know how lucky we are to see the mountain today. Usually it's covered with clouds. That means we'll see stars tonight."

"I can't wait!"

Neither could he.

She started off without him. He paced himself to stay alongside her as they headed for the spot he had in mind to spend the night. They'd bed down in the pines where the air would be fresh and cool.

Along the way she used his field glasses in the hope of spotting the wildlife that flourished on the mountain. After ten minutes of hiking she cried, "Oh, Nik—look at that huge bird!"

He understood her excitement. "I can see it without the binoculars. It's a bearded vulture."

"Bearded?"

"It has a mustache." She giggled like a girl. "That one probably weighs ten pounds.

"I can see why. Its wingspan is enormous."

"Three to four feet across. This is a protected eco-system with multiple climate regions. Some plants and animals here aren't found anywhere else in the world."

Her face lit up. "I'm so glad we came here. I wouldn't have missed a sight like this for the world."

As far as he was concerned, the sight staring up at him had no equal. If there weren't other hikers moving back and forth on the trail, he would have taken her in his arms and kissed the daylights out of her. "This is only the beginning," he murmured. "Come on. Let's get to our destination. I'm hungry. How about you?"

She laughed. "Do you even need to ask?" They

headed out for the tougher part of the climb, but she proved herself equal to the task. Before long they reached the refuge where the climbers could have a meal and a bed for the night.

"One more drink of water will sustain us until we reach the sacred spot."

Her lips curved upward. "Sacred?"

"It *will* be after we've christened it."

"That's an interesting choice of words," she said with a half chuckle before draining the rest of her water bottle.

Nik watched her throat work. Her natural beauty caused every male in the vicinity to take a second and third look. One of the male hikers passing by muttered in Greek to his buddy that Nik had it made for tonight with the dark blonde goddess. Nik ignored him.

For one thing, if he'd been the hiker who'd seen Fran standing there with another guy, he would have wished he'd found her first. For another, he was too happy being with her to take offense at anything.

Again he marveled that despite the tragedy that had struck their family, despite Demi's parentless state, despite the headaches of becoming the new head of the Angelis Corporation, being with Fran felt right and filled the gaping hole inside him. She brought a new sense of purpose to his life that had been missing.

Last night he'd fallen asleep holding the small Atlas in his hands, enchanted by her inimitable charisma and her extraordinary insight. He could wish he'd met her before she'd ever known her husband. But there was no use wandering down that pointless road.

The past needed to stay in the past. She was here now. That's what was important, and she was with Nik.

If she hadn't felt the connection to him growing stronger every minute they were together, she would have flown to the United States today. For now he'd shoved his deepest fear to the back of his mind.

"It's getting dark. Ten more minutes and we can call it a night. Let's go."

She followed him up the trail that had grown even steeper. "I'm surprised we're the only ones not staying there."

He smiled to himself. "They don't have your sense of adventure."

"Too bad we can't climb Mount Athos next."

Nik chuckled. "You mean the Greek mountain forbidden to women?"

"Yes, but it didn't stop the French author Maryse Choisy. Kellie and I read the paperback she wrote."

"Un mois avec les hommes?"

"That's it! *A Month with the Men.* She sneaked into one of the monasteries on the mountain undercover to see how the monks lived. In her words, she turned one of them down. Kellie and I decided she broke his heart."

"More like his pride," Nik theorized.

"To find a woman there, he must have thought he was having a vision."

Nik couldn't resist adding a comment. "She must have found him unappealing, otherwise she might have spent a much longer time there and no book would have been produced."

Suddenly the air was filled with the delightful sound of her laughter. It startled some squirrels who scrambled into the higher branches of a pine tree.

"Let's be thankful we're on Mount Olympus, where

Zeus allowed both male and female gods to romp together in the Elysian fields."

"That must have been something," she quipped. "I always pictured those fields to be white."

"When we're up on top slipping and sliding on the barren summit covered in rocks, you'll learn the truth. I'm afraid mythology has a lot to answer for," he drawled.

"I guess I like reality better."

"Good, because we've arrived at our reality." He headed through the trees, far enough away from the trail so no one would spot them. Soon he came to a small clearing surrounded by pines. Excited to be here, he removed his pack. "In a few minutes I'll have the tent erected and we can eat." He pulled out the big flashlight and turned it on.

"Let me help." After taking off her pack, she pitched right in. They worked together in companionable silence.

"I can tell you've done this before. You're the perfect person to bring on a hike like this."

"Coming from you, I'm flattered. The truth is, I used to camp with my parents and my younger brother, Craig. We usually took Kellie with us. She's a great camper, too. Fearless. We'd go on lots of trips with some of our extended families who loved the outdoors."

Nik digested everything before glancing at her. "I didn't know you had a sibling."

"He died at fifteen of leukemia. I didn't think I'd recover from the loss, but time took the worst of the pain away. One day your pain over losing your sister will fade, too."

The news sobered him. "Tell me about your parents."

"Dad works for a newspaper and has his own political column. My mother still works as an administrator at the school district. I have a lot of aunts and uncles and cousins on both sides. It makes for a big family like yours."

She'd experienced more than her lot of suffering. The death of a loved brother followed by an agonizing divorce… No wonder she had so much depth of character.

"Where have you lived since you've been on your own?"

"In a small condo."

"Not with your parents?"

"No, but it's near my parents' home where I grew up."

"You're more independent than most of the women I know. I admire you for that."

"I could have gone back home, but I need my own space. So do my parents."

They moved inside the tent to lay out their sleeping bags. He reached in another part of his pack for the picnic food they'd purchased before leaving Athens. Salad, fruit, sandwiches and a half dozen pastries.

Nik positioned the light so they could see while they sat across from each other to eat.

"Mmm, this tastes fabulous."

He flicked her a glance. "Have I told you how fabulous you've been today?"

She had to finish chewing before she could talk. "I was just thinking the same thing about you. You're so easygoing. After Rob, I—" She paused for a minute. "I'm sorry. I can't believe I bring up his name so often. Forgive me."

"What is there to forgive? You were married what, three years? It's normal."

"Maybe, but it's rude to you and disrespectful to him."

"A woman with a strong conscience. It's one of the many things I like about you." He popped some grapes in his mouth. "I'm curious about something. Did your parents name you Fran at birth?"

She reached for a morsel of baklava. "No. My legal name is Francesca, but I got kidded about it at school, so I went by Fran."

He frowned. "You were kidded because of it?"

"It sounds too pretentious. I was named for my grandmother on my mother's side."

"How would you feel if I called you Francesca?"

"Why would you do that?"

"Because it appeals to me."

"My parents only called me that when I was in trouble with them."

One eyebrow lifted. "Did that happen often?"

"More than I'd like to admit. In the seventh grade I signed up for a dance class at a local studio with Kellie without thinking about it. When my parents got the bill, they couldn't believe what I'd done. They didn't get mad exactly. Dad said it showed ingenuity, but I was still in trouble for a while."

Nik chuckled.

"And then there was the time we decided to skip our last year of high school and go to a finishing school in France. We wrote to this *pensionnat* as a lark, not thinking we'd get accepted because we applied to the school so late. Wouldn't you know my parents got another letter in the mail, this time from Paris? The directrice informed them she was happy to enroll me in the school and would they please send $2,000 to secure my place.

"Once again I got called to my parents' bedroom and they showed me the letter. I honestly couldn't believe it and told them Kellie and I had just been fooling around."

"But your parents recognized that indomitable spirit in you and they let you go," Nik divined.

"Yes. They felt the experience would be good for me."

"And was it?"

"Yes, after I got over a fierce, two-week bout of homesickness. We had the most awesome adventures of our lives and came back speaking adequate French."

Intrigued, he said, "Did you inherit your candor from your mother or your father?"

"Both my parents, actually." She wiped her fingers on the napkins they'd brought. Now that she'd finished eating, she settled back on the sleeping bag, propping up her head with her hand. "Since you've never married, tell me something. Have you ever lived with a woman?"

"No."

"That sounded final. Then tell me about the latest love interest in the life of the famous Nikolos Angelis. Don't scoff. Your legendary reputation precedes you."

He laughed instead.

"Why didn't you take her camping? I can't think of a better way to get to know someone than on a trip like this."

"Agreed." After putting the leftover food in the bag, he stretched out on his back and put his hands behind his head. "Lena would have pretended to enjoy it for my sake."

"So-o?" She strung the word out.

He turned his head to look at her. "So, I didn't feel like getting to know her better. Does that answer your question?"

Fran sat up looking shocked. "How long did you date her?"

"Twice."

"Does this happen with every woman after you've dated her twice?"

"Sometimes three, but most of the time it happens after one experience."

"You're not kidding me, are you?" she said in a quiet voice.

"No."

"If that's true, then why did you agree to bring *me* camping?"

He turned on his side and moved closer. "You're an intelligent woman. You figure it out."

"You're starting to scare me, Nik."

"Good. It's time you began to take me seriously. Surely it hasn't escaped your notice I'm attracted to you? I did everything I could to prevent you from leaving Athens. No woman has ever caused me to walk out on my family and my job to make sure she didn't get away from me. You must know how much I want you."

"You shouldn't say things like that to me. Our relationship isn't like any other."

"I'm glad you've noticed."

"Please don't come any closer. We'll both regret it if you do."

He cupped the side of her face with his free hand. "Don't pretend you don't want the same thing," he whispered against her lips. "I see it in your eyes. Right now that little pulse in your throat is beckoning me to kiss it."

"No, Nik—"

But he couldn't stop. Consumed by a desire so much greater than he'd known before, he covered her pulse with his mouth, relishing the sweet taste of her velvety skin. When it wasn't enough, his lips roamed her features, covering every centimeter of her face until he found her quivering mouth. Slowly he coaxed her lips apart until she began to respond with a hunger she couldn't hide.

Their low moans of satisfaction mingled as their kisses grew deeper and longer. Like water spilling over a dam, there was no holding back. Time lost meaning while they brought pleasure to each other. He couldn't get enough. Neither could she. When had he ever felt like this in his life? Never.

"You're so beautiful," he murmured, undoing her hair so he could run his fingers through it. "Do you have any idea how long I've been aching to do this?" Nik buried his face in her honey-blond tresses. He couldn't stop kissing her.

When he felt her hands slide into his hair, thrilling chills raced through his body. "Admit you want me, too," he said, out of breath.

"You don't need me to admit to anything," she came back.

"But I want to hear the words." He plundered her mouth once more.

"I'm afraid to get close to you."

"Because your ex-husband hurt you?"

"It's hard to build trust again."

"So I'm condemned without a trial?"

"If that were the case, I would have flown home this morning."

Nik sat up. "Don't you know I would never hurt you?"

"I want to believe that," she said in a tremulous voice.

Her husband had done a lot of damage. He could see this was going to take time. In frustration, he got to his feet. "I have to go outside, but I won't be gone long." He picked up the flashlight and unzipped the front of the tent.

"Nik—"

He swung around. "What is it?"

"Nothing. Just be careful."

Fran's heart thudded sickeningly for fear she'd offended him. She gave Nik five minutes before she left the tent to find him. Though the sky was full of stars, there was only a thumbnail moon. The darkness gave the surroundings a savage look. She walked around trying to get her bearings. "Nik? Where are you?"

"I'm right behind you," came his deep male voice.

She whirled around and almost lost her balance. His hands shot to her shoulders to steady her, but he kept their bodies apart. "Explain to me what went on in your marriage that has made you afraid to be with a man again. To be with me," his voice rasped.

"I—I lost my belief in him," she stammered. "When you give marriage your all, and it fails, the fear that another experience could turn out the same way is immobilizing. It's better not to get one started."

Fran heard his sharp intake of breath. "You're the most honest woman I've ever known, but you haven't told me everything. I want to know what he did to kill your love." His hands tightened on her shoulders. She knew he didn't realize how strong he was.

"I can't."

With a withering sound, he let her go. She had to brace her legs not to fall down. After such a beautiful day, Fran couldn't bear for there to be trouble now, but she was standing on the edge of a precipice. If she caved, she'd plunge headlong into a world where the risk of falling in love with this man would be too great.

She'd been playing with fire since agreeing to spend an evening out with him in the Plaka. Now she'd gotten burned around the edges. Better to escape him with a few scars than stay in Greece to see her whole life destroyed. This situation was no longer solely about Demi.

"Since I suggested this hike, I take full responsibility for our being here, Nik. I'd like us to enjoy the rest of the climb tomorrow. You've been so wonderful to me, I'd be a wretch if I didn't thank you for everything. Do you think it's possible for us to be friends from here on out?"

"No," his voice grated. "The situation is murkier than ever and I don't feel the least friendly toward you. But to honor my indebtedness to you for finding Demi and taking care of her, I'll be your guide until we're off the mountain. If you can't open up to me, then so be it. I'm going to bed."

"Nik—"

"Plan to be up by six. Early morning is the best time to reach the summit." He thrust the flashlight in her hands before he disappeared inside the tent.

She bit her knuckle, hating herself for bringing on this impasse. Out of a sense of self-preservation, she'd stopped things before they'd made love. He'd get over this without a problem. Fran wished she could say the same.

Tonight she'd been shaken by the most overwhelming passion she'd ever known. She'd come close to paying the price to know his possession. It didn't seem possible that after just a short time she was on the verge of giving him whatever he wanted.

After pulling herself together she entered the tent, careful not to shine the light near him. He'd climbed in his bag with his long, hard body turned away from her. Once she'd removed her hiking boots, she got inside hers.

He'd opened the screened window at the top of the tent. She could see the stars he'd promised, but they grew blurry with her tears and she knew nothing more.

"It's time to get going," Nik called to her. She let out a groan because it was still dark. "I'll have breakfast waiting for you when you come out of the tent. We'll leave everything here and pack it up after our descent."

The next two hours proved to be a grueling hike with a taciturn Nik only feeding her vital information when necessary. The trail left the sparse pines and vegetation behind. From there they followed it up a ridgeline all the way to the top. He told her this section was called the Kaki Scala. The narrow path was nothing more than scree and shale, rising straight up.

They finally stopped to drink water. She was panting, but Nik didn't seem the least out of breath. He stayed too fit to be winded by a climb like this.

The peak of Mount Mytikas was still forty-five minutes away. Fran's muscles were clearly aching so badly,

Nik declared they'd opt for Mount Scolio, the second-highest peak. It was only twenty minutes further.

When they arrived, clouds had started to form, blocking out the view of the Aegean. Maybe the elements were delivering an omen. They took some pictures with their cell phones. When she was back home, she'd have them made up so she could pore over them and feast her eyes.

"Thank you for bringing me up here, Nik."

"You're welcome."

He might be civil, but there was no softening him up. Before last night, he would have told her some fascinating tale about the gods who played here and worked their intrigues on each other. She missed that exciting man who'd brought her alive in a way she would never know again. Already she was in mourning for him.

After they signed their names in the register, he suggested they head back. Now that he'd done his duty, she sensed he was anxious to get down the mountain and fly home.

She followed him, but the descent was far from easy. Fran had to be careful where to place her feet on the slippery shale. You could twist an ankle if you weren't careful. She had a feeling that for the next few days, she'd suffer from sore knees more than anything else.

By the time they reached the tent, it looked so welcoming, she went inside and crashed on top of her bag. He paused in the entry to look down at her. She eyed him warily. "I'm worn out. Can we stay here for a half hour to rest before starting back?"

His lips thinned. "You do it at your own risk."

"Nik—please— I can't bear for us to have trouble."

He stood there and drained his water bottle, staring at her the whole time through narrowed eyes. "Has this morning's hike worn you down enough that you're ready to tell me what I want to know?"

She sat up, circling her knees with her arms. "This is so hard for me," she whispered.

"Why?"

The air crackled with tension. He hunkered down to pull some rolls and dried fruit from his pack. Being the decent man he was, he shared them with her.

"Because I want things I don't have and probably never will."

Nik squinted at her. "What kinds of things?"

"You'll mock me when I tell you."

"Try me."

"I ache for the one thing that has eluded me. Mainly, a good marriage and children. I need to put myself in a position where I can meet a man who wants the same thing. When you asked me if I'd consider becoming Demi's permanent nanny, I thought seriously about it before I told you no. Demi is precious and I already love her, but being a nanny would put me out of circulation."

"Fran—"

"I know what I'm talking about," she interrupted him. "You'd have to be a woman to understand. To be the bridesmaid for the rest of my life is too ghastly to contemplate. I still have some good years ahead of me and—"

"Just how old are you?" he broke in, sounding upset. A scowl marred his handsome features.

"Twenty-eight. I know it's not old, but having been married, I feel much older. And let's face it, I'm out of the loop. Since you've never been married, you wouldn't know about those feelings, but they're real, believe me."

He handed her some sugared almonds. "Since you're not an unmarried male, you don't have any concept of what my life is like either. Everyone sees the bachelor who can sleep with any woman he wants with no strings. My life is constantly portrayed as something it isn't and no amount of protests on my part will change it. By that blush on your cheeks, I can see you've had those same thoughts about me."

There was no point in her denying it. "After reading about you in a magazine, I might have entertained certain ideas at first, but no longer."

"Even after I came close to ravishing you last night?"

"Nik—nothing happened that we didn't both want."

"Your honesty continues to confound me."

"Why? Have most of the women you've known been deceitful?"

He put the sack of nuts back in the pack before moving closer to her. "No. The fault lies with me for never giving any of them a chance."

Fran cocked her head. "Tell me what your life has really been like, the one no one knows about."

CHAPTER SEVEN

NIK'S EYES WANDERED over her features. "Like you, I was physically adventurous and logged more than my share of visits to the E.R. for stitches and concussions from water and climbing accidents. My parents drummed it into my head that I had to get top grades or they would forbid me from doing the activities I loved.

"Since I couldn't bear the thought of that, I made deals with them. I would study hard and put in my hours at the company, then I'd be given a reward. As a result, when it came time to play, I played harder than my brothers and enjoyed my girlfriends. I went through a phase of wanting to be Greece's greatest soccer player, then that fantasy faded and I decided I wanted to be a famous race-car driver."

"You believed yourself invincible," she said with a grin.

"With top grades came other rewards. I'd been saving the money I earned, and I traveled to the States and South America. While I was climbing in the Andes I met a guy who was putting an expedition together to climb Mount Everest. When I got back from my trip, I put in for a permit to go with him. That climb changed my life."

"In what way?"

"We got caught in a blizzard and lost two of the men. When they fell, I was pulled away from the ledge. The rope saved me, but I was flung back against the rock wall and ended up with internal damage. At first everyone thought I was dead."

"Nik—"

"I was in the hospital for over two months for a series of surgeries. It took me a year to fully recover and I realized I was lucky to be alive. Like you, I did things sometimes without really thinking of the impact on the family. They'd always given me a wide berth because they knew I couldn't be stopped. It took a force of nature to bring me to my senses."

"So that's the reason you haven't climbed *all* the mountains of your country."

He winked at her. "It's one of them. When I saw the toll my accident took on my parents, I decided I'd better get serious about work. The day I joined my brothers in the upper echelons of our company's business, a lot of my playing ended.

"Despite the gossip, my experiences with women have been sporadic of necessity. I found I liked the work. The stimulating challenge of increasing profits and cutting costs appealed to me in a brand-new way. I dug in to make up for lost time. No doubt that's when I developed my Atlas complex."

"Ah. Now I'm beginning to understand."

"That was five years ago."

"How old are you now?"

"Thirty-four."

"And in that short amount of time you surpassed everyone's expectations to the point that you earned your place at the head of the company. You're young to have so much responsibility, but you've obviously earned it. I'm proud of you and so sorry you lost your sister. The pain must be excruciating."

"You've known that kind of pain, too."

"Yes. But in your case, you have that adorable little Demi who'll always bring joy to you and your family. She's so fun to play with. I'd love to see her again."

In a lightning move he grasped her hands. Slowly, he kissed her palms, sending erotic sensations through her hands to the other parts of her body. "Whenever you talk about her, I can feel this deep wound inside of you. Maybe if you talked about it, you could eventually get over it."

Oh, Nik... She lowered her head, not having counted on his exquisite tenderness.

"Tell me," he urged.

"In my later teens I developed a disease called endometriosis. A lot of women suffer from it. My case was so severe, it prevents me from ever having a child. I'd grown up hoping that one day I'd get married and have a cute little boy like my baby brother, but—"

"Francesca—"

Before she knew it, she was lying in his arms. His embrace opened the floodgates. For a few minutes she sobbed quietly against his shoulder, breathing in the wonderful male scent of him. "I'm sorry," she said at last. "Rob knew about my condition before we married. He told me he was fine with the idea of adoption. I believed him.

"Yet a year later he said he still wasn't ready. Eventually I asked him to go to counseling with me because I wanted a baby. In the first session he blurted that he wanted his own flesh and blood or no children at all. I was enough for him. His admission shattered me."

"Agape mou," Nik whispered, covering her face with featherlight kisses. Fran didn't know what the words meant, but his tone was so piercingly sweet, she nestled deeper in his arms, never wanting to move again.

Nik awakened while Fran was still asleep. Both of them were already emotionally exhausted. The fatigue after their hike had done the rest. They'd slept all afternoon. She was still curled into him with her arm flung across his chest, almost possessively, he thought.

Much as he didn't want to leave her for a second, he knew she'd be stirring before long and they needed dinner. Extricating himself carefully from her arms, he left the tent and hurried down to the refuge. The staff fixed him up with some boxed lunches and drinks.

On the way back, he phoned his helicopter pilot. Nik told him to meet them at the dropoff point at seven the next morning. After hanging up, he checked his phone messages. His father had let him know Demi was doing better.

That was a great relief. Under the circumstances, there was no reason to call him back. Nik was on vacation. Since Fran had pointed out to him that he did his work and everyone else's without thinking about it, he knew she was right.

When he entered the tent, he found Fran on her feet brushing her glorious hair. It flowed around her shoulders. Her smoky-blue eyes lit up when she saw him. "Food—" she cried. "I'm starving. Bless you."

Nik put everything down between their sleeping

bags. "Let's eat and then walk over to the stream for a bath."

Her eyes rounded. "Is it deep enough?"

"Probably not for a full submersion."

"That's just as well because I don't have a bathing suit."

They both sat down to eat. "Don't let that stop you."

She sent him an impish smile. "So you're saying you wouldn't be scandalized if I waded in without it?"

His pulse accelerated. "I would be so overjoyed, I'd probably expire on the spot of a massive heart attack."

"I love the things you say, Nik." Ditto. "Do you suppose the gods wore clothes during their picnics up on top?"

Laughter rumbled out of him. "I never thought about it. I find I'm dazzled by the sight before my eyes right here." Upon that remark, he tucked into his sandwich.

"Kellie thinks you look like a Greek god."

"Then it's a good thing she couldn't see the scars on my midsection when I was holding up the world."

Her smile warmed him in all the hidden places. "I'm sure she was talking about the whole picture. American women, and probably all the other women in existence, have a certain penchant for the authentic Greek-god look. Like I told you in the hospital, it's a good thing Demi inherited her mother's features. As for everything else, she's almost too beautiful to be real. Her black hair and olive skin are still a wonder to me."

"Just as your northern-European blond locks and violet eyes stop traffic over here."

"Just once I'd like to see that happen."

She never took him seriously. "It already did on the hike yesterday."

"What do you mean?"

"There were two guys watching you all the way to the refuge. At one point they stopped. In my hearing they commented I had it made to be with a goddess like you."

"They really called me a goddess?" She laughed in patent disbelief. "Thank you for telling me that. You've made my day." She drank her soda.

"Leandros confided that Kellie was going to find you a husband while you were here. I must say she knew what she was doing when she asked you to take this trip. My helicopter pilot Keiko wasn't able to keep his eyes off of you. As for my brothers..."

"Oh, stop—" She put down her can. "Let's get serious for a moment. Don't you think we should break up camp and head down before it gets dark?"

Without looking at her he said, "Plans have changed. Because we took such a long nap, I phoned my pilot. He'll be waiting for us at the dropoff point in the morning at seven."

He heard her take an extra breath. "In that case I'm going to the stream to take a little sponge bath."

"Do you want any help?"

"I'll call out if I need it."

Nik looked up in time to see the blood flow into her cheeks. She reached for her backpack and stepped outside like a demure maiden who sensed the hunter.

While she was gone, he cleaned up their tent. When she returned, smelling of scented soap and toothpaste and wearing a new blouse, he grabbed his pack and took off. After following the stream to a pool, he stripped and took a real bath.

Half an hour later he rejoined her in a clean T-shirt

and jeans, and found her inside her bag, reading a book with the flashlight. She'd braided her hair. It lay over her shoulder like a shiny pelt, just begging him to undo it. The woman had no idea what she did to him.

Darkness had crept over the forest, sealing them inside. All that was left to do was tuck them in for a summer's night he could wish would go on forever.

He lay down on top of his bag and turned to her. "What are you reading?"

"*The Memphremegog Massacre.* It's about a gruesome murder that takes place in a monastery. But after a day like today, I can't seem to get into it." She put the book down and turned off the light. "You were gone for a while. Any news from home?"

"Yes. My father left a message."

"Problems?" she asked a trifle anxiously

"No. Demi seems to be doing fine."

"Oh, thank goodness. Did you talk to him?"

"No. I took your advice and didn't call him back. I'm on vacation with the first woman I've ever taken on a trip and want to enjoy it."

After a silence, "Are you? Enjoying it I mean?"

"What if I told you that despite everything, I've never been happier?"

"*Nik—*"

"What about you? Are you having a good time?"

He heard her bag rustle. The next thing he knew she wrapped her arm around his neck and kissed him on the lips. "Despite everything, I'm in heaven." She kissed him again all over his face, brows, eyes and nose, as if she really meant it. "I've decided I've been in a dream all this time because no man could be as wonderful as you. Goodnight."

"Don't go to sleep yet," he begged after she let go of him and moved back to her bag. "I need to talk to you."

Something in his voice must have alerted her he was serious because she lifted her head to look at him. "What is it?"

"After you've been so open and honest with me I want you to know the truth about me. Before I was released from the hospital after my climbing accident, the doctor told me I would never be able to give a woman a child."

A minute must have passed, then, "Oh, Nik—" Tears immediately filled her eyes. "If anyone understands what that news did to you, I do. It explains so much," she cried.

He kissed her sensuous mouth. "My injuries were such that I had impaired sperm production. In a flash, any dreams I had of generating my own offspring died. Like you, I had time to come to grips with it.

"But there was a bad side effect. I found myself not getting into serious romantic relationships. If I gave myself to a woman who couldn't handle it, then I feared *I* wouldn't be able to handle it. In a sense I was emotionally crippled."

"I went through the same thing. You've been suffering all this time."

"Though it's true I hadn't found the woman I was looking for up to the point of my accident, the situation was changed after I was released to go home."

"Does anyone else know?"

"Only my doctor, and now you."

She tried to sit up, but he put his hands on her shoulders. "Let me finish. Out of the refiner's fire after losing my sister and her husband, you suddenly appeared in my life, loving my niece. Two miracles happened that day. Demi was found alive and there you were."

"Nik—"

"I don't want you to leave Greece."

"I know."

He jackknifed into a sitting position. "I'm being serious."

"Nik—I thought we were going to forget our cares and enjoy our vacation? You were the one who told me not to think about when it was over, and just take each day as a special gift."

"I can't stop thinking. The idea of you flying back to the States is ruining the trip for me."

A throaty laugh poured out of her. "You're impossible, do you know that?"

"But you still think I'm wonderful."

"Yes. That will never change."

Keep it up, Fran. "How do you know?"

She sighed. "I just do."

"You sound very sure."

"What's this all about? If I didn't know better, I'd think you were worried about something."

"I didn't know I was until you mentioned it."

"Then let's talk about it now."

"Maybe tomorrow."

"That's not fair!" she cried. "So what's going to happen tomorrow?"

"A surprise I can guarantee you'll love."

"And then you'll tell me after?"

"We'll see."

"Will this surprise be hard on the knees?"

He chuckled. "You won't have to lift a finger, let alone a foot."

"Really?"

"Trust me."

"We're going to lie on a beach all day."

"That'll come the next day."

"How about a hint?"

He inched closer to play with her hair. "It has to do with one of your obsessions."

"I don't have any."

"Yes, you do. They come with your spirit of adventure. But now I find I don't want to talk anymore. It's my turn to kiss *you* goodnight."

"I don't think I could handle that right now."

"Good. I like you best when you're a little off kilter. Give me your mouth, Francesca. With or without your capitulation, I need to taste it again."

Her back was still to him as he began kissing her neck, working his way around until he was on the other side of her. He tangled his legs with hers, crushing her to him the way he'd been longing to do. Her mouth seduced him, thrilled him beyond belief. After thirty-four years it was happening.

"I don't think you have any idea what you're doing to me," he murmured feverishly, "but I never want you to stop."

Fran's body gave a voluptuous shudder. "I don't want to stop either. I love the way you make me feel, but this is all happening way too fast and we can't always have what we want."

"Give me one good reason why."

"Because I'll be leaving Greece shortly. I don't want to be in so much pain I can't function after I get home. I don't know about other women, but I'm not able to have a romantic fling and then move on to the next one without giving it a thought.

"You and I met under the most unique of circumstances. I'll never forget you and I'll cherish every moment we've had together, but this isn't right. I take full blame for everything. Your Angelis charm worked its magic on me, but now you have to help me be strong."

Shaken by her words, Nik raised up. "Will you at least agree to see what I've planned for tomorrow before we fly back to Athens?"

"Of course."

Afraid if he kissed her again, he wouldn't be able to stop, he moved as far away as he could. Without her in his arms, the night was going to be endless.

The helicopter was waiting for them in Pironia. With Nik's assistance, Fran climbed on board, having eaten a substantial breakfast at the refuge before their final descent. The sun was already hot, portending one of the sunny days for which Greece was famous this time of year.

She felt the pilot's gaze on her as she took a seat behind him and strapped herself in. He was attractive and wore a wedding ring. Because of Nik's remarks last night she was more aware of him, of everything.

Nik handed her the field glasses. "We're going sightseeing. You'll want those." As soon as he'd fastened himself in the copilot's seat, the rotors whipped the air and they lifted off.

Her stomach lurched. She was okay in the air, but feared she could never get used to the takeoffs and landings. Then she chastised herself for thinking the thought because she'd probably never travel in a helicopter again once she left Athens for home.

Home. Strange how it sounded so remote. Her Grecian adventure with Kellie had turned out to be so much more, she felt as if she'd become a part of the landscape. It seemed as though her world started and ended with him and little Demi. What would life be like when there was no more Nik and that sweet little girl? She couldn't bear to think about it. Couldn't wait to see her and hold her again.

When they'd been flying for a while she leaned forward to ask him a question. "Where are we going? Is it still a secret?"

He turned on the speaker. "We're coming up on a long peninsula on your left. The whole thing is called Mount Athos."

"You're kidding! I mean, you're really taking us there? But women aren't allowed!"

"True, but since you're dying to see it, I'll show it to you from the air."

"Oh, Nik—this is the most exciting thing that's ever happened to me!"

The two men smiled at her enthusiasm, but she didn't care.

"The place is a national treasure, but you already know that after reading about it. Still, to see it like this will give you a greater understanding of why it's called the Holy Mountain. I think it's one of the most beautiful places on earth."

"Have you spent time here?"

"When I turned eighteen, my father brought me and my brothers. To me, it was like a fantasy. The various monasteries dot the landscape. As you will see, some of them are as enormous as castles. My favorite is the Monastery of Saint Docheiariouthe, situated right on the Aegean. The beach is pristine because the monks don't often swim."

"I'm envious of your experience."

"It was something I'll never forget. We walked everywhere, discovering caves that still house religious hermits. Do you know some of the churches have more gold than many countries keep in their vaults? The beauty of their architecture and the icons are something to behold."

"Are the monks all Greek?"

"No. They come from every country in the Orthodox world and even some from non-orthodox countries. You'll notice gardens tended with meticulous care. There's a spiritual atmosphere to the whole place."

"Mountains seem to have that essence, even without monasteries. I felt it yesterday on top of Mount Olympus. During your travels, did you ever climb Mount Sinai?"

"Not yet. Maybe one day. I hear it has monasteries, too."

Her heart ached at the thought of him going there without her.

The pilot dipped down so she could get a bird's-eye view. For the next twenty minutes she feasted her eyes on the marvels passing beneath them. She knew her oohs and aahs amused the men, but she couldn't hold back. The sights were incredible. Nik pointed out his favorite monastery.

"I can see why. The setting against the water is indescribably beautiful." He loved the water.

"If you've had enough, we'll head for Thessalonika."

"I don't think you could ever get enough of this place. Thank you so much for this privilege. Thank you for flying us here in perfect safety, Keiko. I'm in awe of your expertise."

"He's the best at what he does," Nik interjected, while the pilot just smiled.

Before long they landed at the airport's helipad where a dashing black sports car was waiting. Nik walked her over and helped her inside. "I asked my driver to bring my favorite car here so we could drive it back to Athens at our leisure. Keiko will fly our camping gear back." After stowing their packs, he got behind the wheel.

In the next moment he put a hand on her thigh, squeezing gently. It caused her to gasp. "Since the car is carrying precious cargo, I promise I'll keep the speed down."

"How fast can it go?"

"One hundred and ninety-nine miles per hour." After a pause he said, "If you'd rather I rented a car, I'll do it. The decision is yours."

She saw the heightened excitement in his dark eyes and wouldn't have deprived him of this for the world. Besides, she'd never been in a sports car. With Nik, everything was a first, but he didn't need things to add to his remarkable persona. The man himself was the most captivating male on the planet and had a stranglehold on her.

"Well now, darlin'," she drawled with an exaggerated Texas accent. "Why don't y'all show me what a famous race-car driver you really are?"

An explosion of laughter resounded in the car.

She'd said the magic words. He was in his element, and she'd given him permission to enjoy himself. That was one of the things she loved about him. Nik considered her feelings before he did anything. The fact that he always put her first put him in a special class of human beings.

He wasn't a show-off in any sense of the word, which was the reason why she wanted to see him discard his cares and have fun. A second later they wound around to the main road. After the coast was clear, they literally flew down the highway. He flashed her a smile that said he didn't have a worry in the world. It was wonderful to see him this happy after the pain he'd just lived through.

The man seemed to be in heaven, driving with the expertise of any race-car driver she'd ever watched on TV. He infected her with his excitement.

Eventually he had to come to a stop at the intersection for the next town. She turned in his direction. "I'm convinced you could have made it big in the racing world."

Nik eyed her back. "I was tempted, but some newer thrill came along."

"You're like me, always wanting to see what's around the next corner in case I missed out."

"That describes us, Fran. Since you mentioned Mount Sinai, how would you like to climb it with me?"

She blinked. "You mean before I fly home?"

"Why not? Neither of us has ever been there. It'll be a first-time adventure we can experience together."

Fran shook her head. "I couldn't take advantage of you or your generosity like that."

"I think you're afraid I'll take advantage of *you*, so I'll make you a promise. Earlier you asked if we could just be friends and finish our hike to the top of Mount Olympus. I was too frustrated at the time to reassure you. But if you'll give me a second chance, I'd like to spend more time with you. We'll travel there as two friends, nothing more."

Oh, Nik...

"Being with you has made me forget my troubles for a while. I love this feeling of freedom. You're easy to talk to, easy to be with when we don't talk. I'm enjoying your companionship. Can you honestly tell me you don't feel the same way?"

He already knew the answer to that question. How could she say no to him when she knew in her heart he was being totally sincere with her? Since coming away with him, she'd seen and felt how the years had fallen away from him. She'd been given a glimpse of the younger, responsibility-free Nik who had existed before his mountain-climbing accident. With him she felt carefree, too.

They *were* good together. Good for each other. They'd confided in each other and she felt she could trust him. After what she'd told him about trust the other night, that was saying a lot.

"Tell you what. You've convinced me to live dangerously for a little longer."

For an answer, the car shot ahead, leaving her dizzy and reeling. It took zipping along for ten minutes before she could speak. "I hate to tell you this, but you're running high on adrenaline right now."

"But you don't mind," he said with a confidence that seemed part of him.

"No." *I don't mind.* She turned her head to look out the passenger window. Her heart was palpitating so hard in her throat, she couldn't make a sound.

They drove on to the next village where he turned

off the road into the parking lot of a café. After shutting down the motor, he undid his seat belt and turned to her. "I'm going to run inside and get us some food we can eat in the car. Now that we have new plans, I can't get us back to Athens fast enough. You like lamb?"

"I adore it." Her response corresponded with the vibrating sound of his cell phone. "Are you going to answer it?"

He checked the caller ID. "It's from Sandro. That's odd."

"Maybe you'd better get it."

He flashed her another heartstopping smile. "Is that *Mrs. Atlas* talking now?" he teased.

Her soft laughter filled the car as he pulled the phone from his pocket. It was a text message. In the subject line Sandro had put *Emergency.* Nik clicked on to read the message.

Demi started a fever during the night and cries incessantly. Mother hasn't been able to get it down and called the doctor. He told her to bring her to the hospital in Mykonos. We're here now. We don't know if she's come down with a cold, or if she's still suffering from her trauma. She won't eat or drink. I promised Mother I'd keep you informed. She wants everyone here.

Nik pressed Reply.

I'm in my car approximately 160 miles from Mykonos. Should be there within two hours. Have a helicopter standing by at the dock for me. Make sure my driver is there to take care of my car. Keep me posted.

Fran stared at him after he'd pocketed his phone. "Something serious has put those frown lines on your face. Tell me what's wrong."

"Your instincts were right. Demi's back in the hospital."

"Oh, no—" Tears sprang from her eyes. "Not that little darling—"

"She's feverish and won't settle down. I'm afraid Mother's falling apart. Wait here for me. I'll be right back with the food. Sandro will keep us informed if she gets worse."

Fran watched his long, powerful legs eat up the distance and disappear inside. She feared any plans he'd had to take her to Mount Sinai would have to be put on permanent hold. Neither of them could think with little Demi in the hospital again.

Nik was back before she knew it. "I'm glad we're in this car. We ought to make it to the port under two hours. The helicopter will ferry us to the hospital."

She opened the sacks and they helped themselves to food and drink. "Your brothers told me Melina had never had other people tend Demi, so I'm not surprised she's having trouble. Of course she's comfortable around your family, but it was her parents she was bonded to. Obviously this transition is going to take more time than I thought."

"I agree. When we get to the hospital, I'm going to follow through and call a child psychiatrist for consultation. I want another opinion besides the pediatrician's. And there's another possibility. Maybe she has internal injuries like I received on my climb of Everest. Land-ing on her back like that could have damaged a vital organ and she's in pain."

"Just remember she was all right when you took her home."

"Sometimes internal injuries show up later."

"If that's true, then the doctor will find out. She's going to be all right, Nik. That child survived a tornado. She'll survive this. You're all doing everything possible for her."

He grimaced. "What if it's not enough? If our family lost her..."

She touched his arm. "Don't even think it!" But deep inside, Fran was worried about it, too. She adored that baby. This was new territory for all of them. His love for his niece had never been more evident. "I wish I could help you."

"You already have simply by being with me." He grasped her hand, twining his fingers through hers while he drove with his left. But soon he had to let her go to answer another text. They kept coming, feeding them information until they reached the helipad near the ferries.

Nik's driver jumped down and hurried around to the driver's seat while they climbed in the helicopter once more. Nik stowed their backpacks onboard. "We're flying to the hospital in Mykonos."

She sat in her usual spot and buckled up. Her emotions were so up and down, she was hardly cognizant of the takeoff. Fran found herself repeating a new mantra. *Demi can't have anything seriously wrong with her. She just can't.*

It seemed to take forever to reach the island. The pilot set them down on the pad outside the E.R. area of the hospital in the town of Mykonos. Nik helped Fran out, then gathered their backpacks before hurrying inside with her.

"Cosimo said they've got her in a bigger private room for the moment to accommodate the family. It's down this wing."

The second they opened the door, their family descended on Nik as though he was their savior. He was the force they gravitated to because he had that intangible aura that made everyone feel better.

Fran felt terrible she'd said anything to take him away from them. Yet, on the other hand, she'd seen him freed of responsibility for a few days, and he'd become a different man who'd been revitalized.

He turned to Fran. After the others greeted her, he led her over to the crib. Demi lay on her side. An IV had been inserted in her foot. She looked and felt feverish.

"Evidently she's been like this all day," Nik whispered. "Her temp is still too high."

Fran looked at his mother. She was an elegant woman with silvery wings overlaying her short black hair. "Have they done all the tests on her?"

Mrs. Angelis nodded, clutching the railing of the crib. "They can't find anything wrong. The doctor's perplexed."

"Is she asleep?"

"No, but they gave her something to help her rest in order to bring the fever down."

Nik put an arm around his mother's shoulders. "She has to be missing Melina."

His mother's eyes filled with tears. "She was the best mother in the world. It's wicked that she was taken away from us. I feel so helpless. My dearest little Demitra."

"She'll get past this, Mrs. Angelis," Fran assured her, but deep down she was weeping inside to see Demi lying there, limp. It reminded her of the way she'd found her in the bushes. "Homesickness can bring on all her symptoms, but it won't last forever," she said, if only to try and convince herself.

Nik's father, whose salt-and-pepper hair was thinning on top, had come to stand on the other side of the crib. "Of course it won't."

Unable to resist, Fran leaned down and smoothed the black curls with her fingers. "Demi, sweetheart? It's Fran. What's the matter?"

Nik slid his arm around her waist. "Sing to her. Maybe your voice will rouse her."

Fran tried several lullabies, but there was no response. She thought her heart would break and started with another one. All of a sudden Demi's eyes opened and she looked up at Fran. Then she made whimpering sounds and stretched an arm out.

There was a hushed silence in the room. All eyes were on the drastic change in the baby.

"Go ahead and pick her up," Nik murmured.

At his urging, Fran bent over and gathered the baby in her arms. "Well, hi, little sweetheart. Did you just wake up?" She had to be careful because the IV was still attached to her foot.

Demi snuggled in her arms. It was almost as if she was saying she'd missed Fran. The demonstration of affection was too much for Fran who hid her face in the baby's curls for a minute. She kissed her forehead and cheeks. "I've missed you, too. So has your uncle Nik."

She would have handed Demi to him, but he shook his head. "She wants you."

In the periphery she noticed his family. They appeared pretty well dumbstruck. "Let's see if she wants a bottle and will take it from you." He turned to his mother. "Did you bring one?"

"Oh— Yes. There are several in the diaper bag over there on the table."

Nik got one out and brought it to Fran. After pulling a chair over to the crib, he told her to sit and see if Demi wanted any milk.

Fran subsided in the chair and cradled the baby. "Are you hungry, you cute little thing? Would a bottle taste good?" She put the nipple in her mouth, not knowing what would happen.

Gasps of surprise escaped everyone when Demi stared up at Fran with those beautiful brown eyes and started drinking. Nik's exhausted-looking parents smiled at her with tears in their eyes. The relief on their faces spoke volumes. His brothers were so joyful, they squeezed Nik's shoulder.

Fran was tongue-tied and glanced up at Nik. "I honestly don't know why Demi responds to me."

His dark eyes were suspiciously bright. "You rescued her from the garden and were the first person to show her love when she came back to life. I don't think we need to look for any other answer than that. Do you?" He stared first at her, then around at his family.

His father wiped the wetness off his cheeks. "Our only problem now, *Kyria* Myers, is to convince you to stay with us a while until Demi feels comfortable again with everyone."

"She went downhill after you and Nik left the island," his mother volunteered. "Please stay." Her heart was in her voice.

Conflicted by her fear of what was happening here, Fran couldn't look at them.

"What do you say?" Nik was still leaving it up to her. She loved him for that.

CHAPTER EIGHT

"OF COURSE I'LL STAY."

As if Fran needed to be convinced...

Demi had caught at her heart the second she'd seen her lying in the bushes. She might be Nik's flesh and blood, but Fran loved her, too. "It'll be no penance to help out."

He squeezed her shoulder, filling her with a new kind of warmth. "I'll tell the doctor. As soon as he releases her, we'll all drive home together." Near her ear he whispered, "We'll do the Sinai climb later."

No. They wouldn't. But it was a beautiful thought she'd cherish forever.

Within fifteen minutes they were able to leave the hospital. It was decided Fran would be wheeled outside holding Demi so there was no chance the baby would revert back to hysterics.

The family had come in two cars. Nik helped her into the back of his parents' car before sliding in next to her. His brothers followed in one of their cars. The whole scene was so surreal, Fran had to pinch herself.

Anyone seeing her would think she was a new mother, except that Demi was too big and her coloring was the opposite of Fran's. Still, she imagined this was how a new mother felt taking her baby home for the first time. How she wished Demi were really hers! Babies were miracles, and this one happened to be the miracle baby everyone in Greece was talking about.

When they reached the villa, Nik carried their backpacks to the suite where she'd stayed before. "Let's bathe her."

"I was just going to suggest it."

They worked in harmony. He got everything out she would need to bathe the baby in the tub. Nik filled it. Together they washed her hair and played with her. Demi loved it and kicked her legs.

"That's it, Demi. Kick harder." With his encouragement, she splashed water in her face, but she didn't cry. They both burst into laughter.

"Aren't you a brave girl!"

After wrapping her up in a towel, Nik carried her into the bedroom and laid her down on the bed. Fran sprinkled some powder, then put on her diaper and a summery sleeper. Nik dried her hair and brushed the curls.

"It's time to take her temperature. I'll get the thermometer." Fran hurried over to the dresser. "Here—" She handed it to Nik.

"This isn't going to hurt, Demi." Fran held her breath while he checked it. A few more seconds and he glanced up. "Ninety-nine degrees."

"Wonderful! You're almost back to normal." She kissed the baby's tummy, producing gurgle-like laughter.

"Let's take her out to the patio. When everyone sees how happy she is, they'll all stop worrying and get a good night's sleep." Nik picked Demi up and they walked through the villa and out the doors. Twilight was upon them, the mystical time of evening that gave the island a special glow.

This time the family didn't reach for Demi. They let Nik take charge. He sat down on the swing holding the baby on his lap and patted the spot next to him for Fran. "Her temperature is down. She's had her bath and is ready for bed. You'll be glad to know Fran has agreed to stay here for a few days to help out. Hopefully it won't take long for life to get back to a new normal."

"Demitra isn't the same baby we drove to the hospital this morning," his mother remarked. She eyed Fran. "It's absolutely uncanny how she responds to you. We're thankful you didn't leave Athens yet."

Fran felt it incumbent to explain. "Before the tornado touched down, Kellie and I were on our way to hike Mount Olympus."

"Ah—you like to climb? So does our Nikolos."

"I found that out. Since Kellie wasn't well, he took me to the top. And this morning we flew in the helicopter over Mount Athos."

"An intriguing place," Nik's father interjected.

"For you men," Fran teased. Everyone chuckled.

Nik flicked her a glance with the private message that he looked forward to their climb of Sinai. She got a fluttery sensation in her chest.

"We were up early and then had a long drive back. If you'll forgive us, we're going to put Demi down and we'll see you in the morning."

His father nodded, but Fran saw the speculative gleam in his eyes as they got up to leave. Their family knew Nik never spent this much time with a woman. She could tell his brothers were equally curious about what was going on, though they made no comment. They'd be even more surprised if they learned she and Nik had been on the verge of flying to Egypt.

"Nik? I can tell your parents want to talk to you. Why don't you let me take over from here and give her a bottle?" She drew the baby out of his arms.

"Don't count on me being long."

"Take all the time you need."

Fran was glad to escape to her suite. She disappeared down the hall to the nursery and sat in the chair next to the bed to feed Demi a bottle. Once she'd sung a few songs, the baby fell asleep much faster than Fran would have thought. Maybe there was still a little of the sedative in her system. Between that and her exhaustion, she'd no doubt sleep through the night.

Fran tiptoed out of the nursery and checked her own phone. She found two text messages. One from her mom who wondered how she was doing. Fran hadn't had a chance to tell her anything yet. The other one came from Kellie.

I've been trying to reach you for two days. What's going on? Why haven't you phoned?

Fran checked her watch. It would still be early afternoon in Philadelphia. While she waited for Nik to come, she decided to phone her friend.

"Kellie?"

"Thank goodness it's you, Fran. I was beginning to worry."

"I'm sorry. So much has happened since you left Athens, I hardly know where to start. But before I talk about me, I have to know how you're doing. By now your aunt and uncle have been told everything."

"Yes, and they're being so wonderful to me." Fran heard tears in her voice.

"What about Leandros? Is he still there?"

"No. I told him to leave, but I promised to call him when I was ready to talk. He finally gave up and flew back to Athens."

Fran sank down on the side of the bed. She was sick for both of them. "Are you feeling all right physically? No more fainting spells?"

"No. My aunt says she's going to fatten me up."

"You *have* lost a few pounds since Easter."

"Enough about me. How soon are you coming home?"

Fran took a deep breath. "Not for a while."

"How come?"

Her hand tightened on the phone. "The baby was in the hospital again with a high fever."

"You're not serious."

"I wish I weren't. She's missing her parents and the family has been at their wit's end."

"Does Demi still reach out to you?"

Fran wasn't about to lie to her. "I'm afraid so. Their family is really hurt by it. None of us can figure it out. Since we brought her back to the villa, her temp is already down. It's uncanny."

"Has Nik—"

"No, Kellie," Fran broke in, reading her thoughts. "He's never mentioned the word *nanny* again. Tomorrow he's going to consult with a psychiatrist to find out what could be going on with Demi. I've promised to stay that long."

"Oh, Fran... Why didn't you come home on the flight Leandros arranged for you?"

Good question. "Because Nik volunteered to take me up on the top of Mount Olympus before I went home."

After a pregnant silence, "Did you go?"

"Yes. On the descent he got a call that Demi was back in the hospital." A little lie that could be forgiven.

"She's his number one priority. I was there before, during and after the funeral. It's clear he put Melina on a pedestal and would do anything for her. I learned he was instrumental in getting her and Stavros together. Did you know Nik was in a bad mountain-climbing accident?"

"He told me."

"Did he also tell you Melina took it upon herself to be at his bedside both in and out of the hospital? Her devotion to him was praised at the funeral."

Fran's eyes closed tightly. She didn't know that.

"If you stay any longer, you'll end up taking care of the baby. It's his way of paying back Melina."

Fran didn't believe Nik had a hidden agenda, not after the rapturous few days together when they'd both opened up their hearts. But she couldn't dismiss the nagging possibility Kellie was right in one regard. Fran was still in Greece of her own free will with no date set to go home yet. Demi's tug on her was growing stronger. *So was Nik's.*

"Are you still there? Are you listening?"

"Yes." She'd been listening to Kellie spill out her broken heart since coming to Greece. Her friend's agony went fathoms deep and colored her thoughts where Fran's relationship with Nik was concerned.

"Remember that old cliché about blood being thicker

than water? It happens to be true. Believe me, I know. After marrying Leandros, I have proof."

In Kellie's mind, Karmela had turned her marriage into a threesome. Maybe there was some truth in it, but Fran knew there had to be a lot more going on. Kellie had a hard time talking about her deepest fears. Fran doubted she'd talked to Leandros about them.

"Do you hear what I'm saying, Fran?"

"Yes." She would have said more, but she heard a noise. Nik had entered the bedroom and shut the door. Turning her back to him she said, "Forgive me, Kellie, but something has come up and I'll have to call you later. I promise."

She hung up and turned around. "I was just returning Kellie's call."

Nik stood at the end of the bed with his hands resting on his hips in a totally male stance. "Is she all right now that she's with her aunt and uncle? She was raised by them, right?"

"Yes. Physically she's fine, but emotionally, I've never seen her so completely devastated. Leandros is back in Athens."

He rubbed his chest absently. "I'm sorry to hear that, especially when it appears her pain has rubbed off on you."

Fran was gutted by her conversation with Kellie. "I have to admit I'm worried about them."

"I'm sorry. Under the circumstances I'll say goodnight and see you in the morning. After breakfast we'll take Demi out in the sailboat. She loves it. Hopefully while we're enjoying ourselves, the doctor will get back to me with some ideas, and we'll go from there."

"I'd like that. Good night, Nik."

Much to her chagrin she wanted him to grab her and kiss her senseless, but he was a man of his word and made no move toward her. Instead, he tiptoed into the nursery. She watched from the doorway as he leaned over the crib to touch Demi's hair. The sweet moment moved her to tears before he came back out.

His eyes looked like glistening black pools in the semidarkness. "*Kalinitha*, Fran."

A light breeze filled the sail. With the surface of the blue Aegean shimmering like diamonds, Fran felt she'd come close to heaven. "Where are we headed, Nik?"

He manned the rudder with the same expertise he did everything else. In bathing trunks and a T-shirt that revealed his hard-muscled body, he looked spectacular.

"Delos. It's that tiny, barren island you can see from here, only three miles away. The Ionians colonized it in 1000 BC and made it their religious capital. There's a specific reason I'm taking us there."

Fran had been holding Demi since they'd climbed onboard. They were both dressed in sun suits and hats. Fran wore her bathing suit underneath. When it got too hot, she'd take the baby below for a nap. "Is there a statue of Atlas? If so, I want to take a picture."

He grinned, dissolving her insides. "Sorry to disappoint you. He resides far away in North Africa."

"Of course. The Atlas Mountains. I'd forgotten. That explains your affinity for them."

"Maybe," he teased. "I'm afraid Delos is the birthplace of Apollo and Artemis, but that's not what's so interesting."

She kissed Demi's cheek. "We're all ears, aren't we, sweetheart?"

"At one point, the island was so sacred, no one was allowed to be born there or die there."

"You're kidding!"

"Those who were about to leave this world, or get ushered in, were rushed off to the nearby islet of Rinia."

She laughed. "Sometimes you just can't stop either one from happening."

"Somehow they managed."

"Sounds like shades of the rules on Mount Athos."

"I was waiting for you to make that connection. At least here on Delos, males and females can go ashore and walk around the ancient ruins."

"What about children? Are they permitted?"

"Yes, but Demi will have to wait until she's six or seven. This afternoon we'll just circle the island. While all the other tourists from Mykonos scramble around, we'll be able to sit back and see many of the remains from the deck."

"It's a glorious day out for sightseeing."

"With this light breeze, my favorite kind."

She felt his gaze linger on her, overheating her in a hurry. "What's the name of your boat? I can't read Greek."

"The *Phorcys*."

"A mythological creature?"

"To be sure. I was raised on the myths. When I was a boy I made up my mind that when I was old enough to buy my own boat, I'd name it for the ancient sea god who presides over the hidden dangers of the deep."

"That sounds exactly like something the protective Atlas would do."

Laughter rumbled out of his chest.

"Does he look like you?"

"Tell you what. One day I'll bring you to Delos alone." *Don't say things like that, Nik. In a few days I'll fly home and never come back here again.* "We'll walk up to the highest point on the island where I'll show you an ancient mosaic of him. He's a gray-haired, fish-tailed god with spiky crab-like skin and forelegs who carries a torch."

"Oh dear. He must have done an excellent job of keeping everyone away." They were getting closer to the island now.

"He did better than that," Nik quipped. "With his wife, Ceto, they created a host of monstrous children collectively known as the Phorcydes."

"That's terrible! How sad they never had a child as beautiful as Demi." Fran shifted the baby to her shoulder and hugged her. "If the gods did exist, they'd be jealous of Melina's daughter. Even without them, she'll need to be guarded well."

And Nik would see to that.

She lifted the binoculars he'd given her to examine the various archaeological sites studded with temples and pillars. Demi reached out to touch them, of course. The action pulled off Fran's hat, which in turn pulled her hair loose from its knot. "You little monkey." She kissed her cheeks and neck, giving up on the binoculars for the moment.

For the next hour they slowly circled the island, but most of the time Fran simply played with the baby who stood up with her help and bounced when Nik talked to her. The baby babbled a lot, causing both of them to laugh.

"She's happy and says she wants to go ashore."

"I know you do, *Demitza*, but you can't have everything you want." Fran loved the way he talked to her.

"I think it's getting too hot for her, Nik. I'd better take her below."

"Go ahead while I drop anchor in this little cove, then I'll join you and we'll have an early dinner."

Fran carried Demi down the steps to the bedroom and changed her diaper. Once she'd put her in a little stretchy suit, she walked her into the galley to feed her. Nik had brought her swing along. It worked as a high chair.

"I bet you're thirsty. I'll fix you a bottle of water first." The baby drank some eagerly. "What would my little princess like for lunch? How about lamb and peaches?"

She grabbed some bottled water for herself and sat down to feed Demi. After a minute Nik appeared. With his olive skin, it didn't take much exposure from the sun to turn him into a bronzed god.

"There's nothing wrong with her appetite," he observed, reaching for a water, too. He sat down next to the baby and watched the two of them. In such close quarters, Fran could hardly breathe because of his nearness. She felt his warmth and smelled the soap he'd used in the shower earlier.

"If you want to finish feeding her, I'll get the food out of the fridge." Anything to keep busy so she wouldn't concentrate on him to the exclusion of all else.

Demi obviously adored Nik and thrived on his attention. Between his smiles and laughter, she couldn't help but be charmed by her uncle. Nik would make a wonderful father one day. Demi was lucky to have him in her life. Just how lucky, she had no idea.

Fran put their meal on the table—salad and rolls, fresh fruit, pastries and juice. A feast.

"This is delicious." She smiled at him. "I see there's nothing wrong with your appetite either." He'd eaten everything in sight.

"That's because you're with Demi and me. We thrive under the right conditions."

"If you'll notice, I ate all my food, too," she admitted.

He flashed her a penetrating glance. "I noticed." After wiping the corner of his mouth with a napkin, he got up from the table. "Come on, little one. It's time to sleep." He picked up the swing with her in it and carried it into the bedroom.

Fran followed with a bottle of formula. Once he'd turned on the mechanism that started it swinging, she handed her the bottle. Demi looked up at them and smiled the sweetest smile Fran had ever seen before she started drinking.

Nik moved Fran over to the bed a few feet away. "We'll have to stay here until she goes to sleep, so we might as well make ourselves comfortable."

She lay down on her side, facing the baby. Nik moved behind her and put his arm around her waist. His sigh filtered through her hair splayed over the pillow. "This is what I call heaven."

They stayed that way without moving. Fran was so content in his arms, and the sound of the swing had a hypnotizing effect on her. When she looked at Demi, the little darling had fallen asleep.

Fran suspected the gentle rocking of the boat had put Nik to sleep, too. But in that regard she was mistaken. In an unexpected motion he rolled her over so she was half lying on him. "Sh-h," he said against her lips before his hungry mouth covered them in a long, languid kiss that went on and on, setting her on fire.

Her need of him was so all-consuming, she couldn't hold back her desire. For a time she felt transported.

"I know I promised I'd treat you like a friend," he whispered in a husky voice, "but it won't work. I can't stop what I'm feeling." He was actually trembling. "I've never wanted any woman in my life the way I want you." His fingers tightened in her hair. "Before I forget all my good intentions, you'd better hurry up on deck while you can. I'm giving you this one chance before all bets are off for good."

Something in his ragged tone told her he meant what he said. If she stayed here a second longer, there'd be no going back and it would be her fault, not his. It shocked her that he had more control than she did.

But when she finally found the strength to move off the bed and get to her feet, she heard him groan. It almost sent her back into his arms until she saw Demi lying there in the swing. Fran's gaze took in both of them.

Neither of them will ever be yours. Go upstairs now, Fran.

She didn't remember her feet touching the ground. When she reached the deck, she threw off her sundress and dove into the water. It was late afternoon now, when the sun was its warmest near the shore. Delightful. But the wonder of it was wasted on Fran who swam around while she struggled with the war going on inside of her.

Should she engage in one mad moment of passion at the age of twenty-eight, then have to live out the rest of her life tortured by the memory? Or should she do the smart thing and avoid the fire? It meant she'd never know joy. Either option was untenable. Thank goodness for the water that hid her tears.

When she finally started back to the boat, she discovered Nik on deck holding Demi. She swam over to the side. "Demi?" she called out and waved her arm. "Can you see me?"

"She's squirming to jump in with you."

A different man had emerged from the bedroom. This one was calm and collected, her urbane host until she left Greece. She died inside, knowing the other one wouldn't make a second appearance. As he'd said, he'd give her one chance. Fran hadn't taken it in order to avoid sabotaging her own happiness. Now she had to pay the consequences.

"The water's wonderful. I'll come onboard so you can cool off."

Nik would never cool off. He'd come down with a fever when he'd first met Fran. With each passing day it had climbed higher until he was burning up. He'd already taken a big swim that morning in cooler water before anyone was up. It had done nothing to bring down his temperature. There was only one antidote, but the thought of it not working terrified him.

Afraid to touch her, he let her climb onboard by herself. She put on her sundress over her yellow bikini. Her movements were quick, but not quick enough. At the sight of her beautiful body, he practically had a heart attack. With Demi in her swing, he could unfurl the sail and raise the anchor.

She hunkered down next to the baby and kissed her, then looked in his direction. "Don't you want to swim?"

"Maybe tonight. I'd prefer to take advantage of the

evening breeze on the way back. Mother will be missing Demi by now."

"Of course. How long did she sleep?"

"Until five minutes ago."

"She doesn't act like she's hungry yet. I think I'll hold her for a while."

Fran couldn't keep her hands off the baby. She walked her over to the bench and sat down with her, giving her kisses on her tummy that made Demi laugh. While she was preoccupied, Nik set sail for Mykonos and guided them toward the villa. By seven-thirty, he brought the boat around and it glided gently to the dock.

In a few minutes he helped her out of the boat with Demi and followed with the swing. No one was on the patio yet. That was good. At the top of the steps he put the swing down and they entered the villa without passing any family members who might pick up on the tension between them.

"I'll start Demi's bath," Fran called over her shoulder. "When she's dressed, you can take her to your mother."

"Good. I'll pick out an outfit." He opened the cupboard and reached for a sundress. In the drawer he found some white stockings and little matching shoes. He put everything on the bed. When he peered in the bathroom, Fran had just finished washing the baby's hair.

She looked up. "Demi's such an easy baby, she's a joy."

"She has Melina's nature."

When Fran lifted the baby from the water, he grabbed a towel and wrapped her in it before carrying her into the bedroom. For just a moment it hit him that his sister really was gone. Tears stung his eyelids. He hugged the baby to him while he fought to regain his composure.

"It's all right to cry, Nik," Fran murmured gently. "Even Atlas has do it once in a while. The problem is, emotion catches up with you when you least expect it. I know what that's like. Even if it's a horrible adage, the pain will ease with time."

He lifted his head. "I'll keep that in mind." Nik lay the baby on the bed and dried her hair.

"Oh—what a darling outfit!"

"I bought it for her several months ago, but it was too big at the time."

"Now it's the perfect size! With her skin she'd look beautiful in any color, but I dare say peppermint pink trumps them all." She held it up in front of Demi. "Don't you love it, sweetheart? Your uncle picked this one out especially for you."

The baby got all excited and touched the hem. Warmed by Demi's reaction, Nik's crushing sense of loss faded. He got busy powdering and diapering her. Fran's eyes shimmered a violet blue as she handed the dress to him. "You do the honors."

"When I bought this, I never dreamed I'd be the one putting it on her." His fingers fumbled with the two buttons in the back. Fran helped the baby to sit up so he could fasten it. Then she put the stockings and shoes on her tiny feet.

"One more minute while we comb her hair." Fran dashed over to the dresser for it. "She has a head of natural curl. What a lucky girl." Nik watched her style it to perfection. "There you go." She kissed her on both cheeks. "Now you're all ready to go see your *yiayia* and *papou.*"

"How did you know those words?" She continually surprised him in wonderful ways.

"I've been listening to the children talk. In France I used to walk through the park near our school and practice my French with them. They make terrific teachers, *Kyrie* Angelis."

To hear her speak any Greek excited him no end. "I'm impressed."

"Why don't you take Demi to find your folks? I'll hurry and shower so I'll be available if you need me. But I'm hoping she had such a good time with us, she'll be able to enjoy her grandparents without me before she has to go to bed."

Nik left the room carrying Demi and found his parents in the living room talking with Stavros's parents. He'd been so focused on his own pain, he'd forgotten they mourned their son and needed Demi's love, too. Four pairs of eyes lit up when they saw their granddaughter decked out like a little princess. For the next few minutes he sat with them while the baby was passed around. Dinner was about to be served. They gravitated to the patio where the rest of the family had congregated.

He put Demi in her swing with a fresh bottle of formula and told them he'd be back. On the way to his apartment he swung by Fran's. There was something he had to say to her, and he couldn't put it off any longer.

"Fran?" He knocked on her door.

His breath caught when she opened it wearing a pair of pleated tan pants and a white blouse. Fresh from the shower, she'd fastened her damp hair at the back of her head with a clip. She'd picked up some sun and wore no makeup, except a frosted pink lipstick, because she didn't need any.

"I take it Demi's all right so far."

"I left her on the patio with the family. We'll see how she does. Before I shower and change, I need to talk to you. It's important. May I come in?"

"Of course."

He shut the door with his back and lounged against it. "What happened on the boat made me realize I can't go on this way any longer."

Fran stood a few feet away from him, rubbing her hips with her palms in a nervous gesture. "Neither can I. While I was showering I came to the decision that I have to leave in the morning, no matter what."

"I have another solution."

"There's isn't another one."

"There is, but I've hesitated to mention it because we've only known each other a week. I want you to marry me."

"Marry?"

The world spun. She turned clumsily and sank down on the side of the bed before she fell. Kellie's warning rang in her ears. *He'll do anything to get you to take care of Demi.*

"You don't want to marry me," she whispered.

"You're terrified again."

She looked away from him. The nerve palpitating at the base of her throat almost choked her. "You know the thrill will wear off."

"I've never been married, but you have. That's your bad experience talking."

"Be serious, Nik."

"I don't know how to get any more serious. I just asked you to be my wife and am waiting for an answer."

She kneaded her hands. "You're not thinking clearly. For one thing, I can't give you children."

"That goes for both of us. We'll adopt."

"That's what Rob said."

"Don't you dare compare me to your ex-husband," he ground out. "To prove it to you, we'll get the adoption papers ready in my attorney's office before the wedding ceremony. The second it's over, he'll get the process moving with the quickest speed possible."

She shook her head. "You don't know what you're saying."

"But I do because I've found the right woman for me." He cupped her face in his hands. "I'm in love with you, Francesca Myers. I can't honestly tell you when it happened, but the point is, it's finally happened to me. I believe it's happened to you, too, but you're too frightened to admit it yet."

Before she could take a breath, he lowered his head and closed his mouth over hers, giving her a kiss that was hot with desire. *A husband's kiss with the intent to possess.* When he finally let her up for air, he pressed his head to her forehead while he tangled his fingers in her hair. "I can't let you leave Greece. We belong together. You know it, and I know it."

Tears ran down her cheeks. "You say this now, but you might not always feel this way."

"I'm not Rob," he bit out. "Your ex-husband did a lot of damage to you, but he's not representative of most males I know, and certainly not of me."

She wiped away the moisture with her fingers. "You've overwhelmed me, Nik."

"Sorry, but it's the way I'm made. Up on Mount Olympus, you told me I was wonderful and you'd never change your mind about me. Was that a lie?"

A ring of white circled his lips, revealing his vulnerability. It was a revelation to her. "You know it wasn't."

"Then prove it and tell me what I want to hear."

She bit her lip. "I need to think about it, Nik."

His jaw hardened. "You still don't trust me?"

"It's not that. I can hardly trust the situation. As I told you in the tent, this is all happening too fast."

"How long did it take your father before he knew he wanted to marry your mother?"

She half laughed through her tears. "Mother rear-ended him in a parking lot at the college. When he got out of the car, pretty furious about it, she ran up to him full of apologies. He said one look in her eyes and he was a goner."

Nik kissed her lips. "My parents had a similar experience when they first met. It happens to lots of couples. Why not us?"

"But our circumstances are different. I've been married, and you haven't. You deserve to start out with a single woman who has no past. I'm a has-been."

"So am I. Don't forget my legion of women I've left in the dust."

"How could I possibly forget them?" she croaked.

He hugged her to him. "I'm madly in love with *you* and everything that formed you into who you are. That includes warts, Rob and Kellie, who won't want me for her best friend's husband."

"I'm afraid she won't while her marriage is in trouble. Oh, Nik—" She flung her arms around his neck and sobbed.

"Am I getting my answer yet?" he whispered into her hair.

She eventually lifted her head and stared at him without flinching. While she had the courage, she needed to ask him something. Her whole life's happiness depended on his answer.

"Nik— Try to be baldly honest with me because I'm going to ask you a hypothetical question."

"Go on."

"If we'd met under different circumstances and there'd been no Demi, do you think you would have asked me to marry you?"

An eerie silence crept into the room. He didn't move a muscle, but she sensed his body go rigid. Instead of the look of desire she'd always seen in his eyes when he was around her, he scrutinized her as though she were an unknown species of insect under a microscope. The longer he didn't say anything, the more fractured she felt.

"What kind of a hold does Kellie have on you that she could turn you into someone I don't know?"

"This has nothing to do with Kellie."

"The hell it doesn't." His wintry voice hit her like an arctic blast, prompting her to fold her arms to her waist. "Tell me what she said to you."

"She's been worried you'd do anything to get me to take care of Demi."

His face morphed into an expressionless mask. "I guess we'll never know if she spoke the truth or not, will we?"

Following his delivery to its ultimate conclusion, a gasp escaped her lips.

"Your advice to let my family come up with solutions has produced fruit. Ever since the funeral they've been in the process of looking for a nanny and expect to interview some candidates as early as tomorrow. For that, I thank you.

"However, you won't be among the prospects because you'll be on a plane flying out of Mykonos airport in the morning to join your best friend in the States where you came from. I hope you'll both be very happy together. Since I don't expect to see you again, I'll say goodbye now."

He was out the door so fast, she was incredulous.

What have I done?

Absolutely panicked, Fran wanted to run after him, but she didn't know where to go to find him. Doing the only thing she could do under the circumstances, she picked up the house phone. Nik had told her the housekeeper would answer.

When she did, Fran asked her if she could find either Sandro or Cosimo and tell them to come to the phone. In a few minutes, Cosimo came on the line.

Without preamble she said, "I hate to disturb you, but I—I'm afraid Nik and I just had words," she stammered. "I *have* to find him."

"I just saw him leave the villa."

Her heart plunged to her feet. "Do you know where he was going? I have to talk to him, Cosimo. It's a matter of life and death to me."

After a distinct pause he said, "He was headed for the marina. When he's stressed, he spends the night on his sailboat away from everyone, but don't tell him I told you that."

"I swear I won't. Bless you."

CHAPTER NINE

NIK RAN TO THE BEACH. After tossing his T-shirt on the sand, he plunged into the water and swam out to his boat moored on the other side of the dock. It was a good distance away, but it was the workout he needed.

He'd never been one to turn to alcohol, but he'd never been this gutted. When he reached the boat, he'd drink until he passed into forgetfulness. If the gods were kind, he wouldn't wake up.

The same stars that had lighted the sky above their tent on Mount Olympus now mocked him as he torpedoed through the water to his destination. When he rounded the pier, he heaved himself over the side of his boat.

A moonlight sail in calm seas sounded perfect. When he was far away from shore, he'd drop anchor and stretch out on the banquette with a bottle of Scotch. With the canopy of the heavens to keep him company, he'd drink himself into oblivion. Always one for adventure, who knew if it wouldn't be his last…

He went down the steps to the galley and rummaged in the cupboard till he found the bottle he was looking for. No glass was needed. Back up on top, he undid the ropes, then walked toward the outboard motor. It would take the boat beyond the buoy. If the wind didn't pick up, it didn't matter.

As he leaned over to turn it on, he thought he heard a voice call out, but the sound coincided with the noise from the motor. It was probably a gull. He put the throttle at a wakeless speed. The boat inched away from the dock. When he was young, he used to pretend he was a thief on the boat, sneaking away into the night.

That's what he felt like right now. Sneaking to a place where he could get away from the pain.

There went that cry again, stronger this time. That wasn't a bird. It was human! He cut the motor.

"Nik—"

It sounded like Fran. Was he hallucinating when he hadn't tasted a drop of Scotch yet? His head shot around behind him. He saw a form doing the breast stroke, trying to catch up.

"Wait for me!" she cried.

Galvanized into action, he slipped over the boat and swam to her. She practically collapsed in his arms while he trod water with her. "Put your head back and take deep breaths."

Her arms tightened around his neck. "I'm all right." Her lips grazed his cheek. "I was afraid you'd l-leave. I couldn't let that happen before t-talking to you first."

"Come on. Let's get you onboard and into some dry clothes. Your teeth are chattering. Let me do the work."

In no time he'd helped her up over the side. She'd plunged in the water wearing the same pants and blouse she'd had on earlier. With her hair streaming down, she looked like a shipwreck victim plucked out of the sea, albeit one more beautiful than he could begin to describe.

He gritted his teeth. "You could have broken your neck."

"But I didn't."

Nik helped her down to the galley and pushed her into the shower. "Take off everything. I'll leave a towel and robe hanging close by."

"Th-thank you."

After he'd found the desired articles for her, he went back up to weigh anchor, then he headed down to his bedroom. Luckily he kept a pair of sweats and a T-shirt onboard. He removed his swimsuit and got dressed.

While he waited for her, he made coffee for both of them. Having a sweet tooth, he added an extra amount of sugar to both mugs. She'd need it after her workout.

Right now he chose not to think about why she'd come. The fact that she'd put herself in jeopardy to catch up to him would do for starters. The rest could come after she was fully revived.

A few minutes later she appeared in the tiny kitchen in his blue toweling bathrobe. Her freshly shampooed hair had been formed into a braid. She smelled delicious. He handed her the coffee which she drank with obvious pleasure.

"Oh, that tastes good."

He lounged against the counter sipping his. "How did you know I was out here?"

"I ran after you. Cosimo saw me and volunteered to stay by Demi. I raced as fast as I could, but you move like the wind. Kind of like the way you drive your car. That was a thrill of a lifetime for me."

"I was in a hurry," he muttered.

"I know. It was all my fault. Every bit of it. Forgive me. Kellie never used to be like this, but the problems in her marriage have made her so unhappy, she doesn't see anything working out for herself, or me."

"Their situation isn't ours."

"You think I don't know that?" She put the mug down and grasped both his arms. "She jumped to all the wrong conclusions from an outsider's perspective, but she lost sight of one thing. I love you, Nik. You have no idea how much." She slid her arms around his neck. "Help me, darling. I can't reach your mouth and I need it more than I need life."

Not immune to her pleading, he picked her up and carried her to his bedroom. But after laying her down, he sat beside her. She tried to pull him down. "Nik—you have to forgive me," she implored him.

His eyes smarted. "I'm the one who needs forgiveness. I fell in love with you the moment we met, then panicked because you were leaving on a trip with Kellie. I had to think of a way to keep you in Greece so we could get to know each other. I used Demi shamefully as my excuse."

"I can't believe it!" she cried for happiness.

"On our camping trip, I was building up the courage to tell you about my medical problem when you told me about yours. After that I couldn't hold back. On our drive home, I would have asked you to marry me, but then we got that call about Demi."

"But I almost ruined everything with that awful question." She broke down in tears. "Please forgive me, Nik."

"I think I like this ending better. To watch you swim toward my boat as if your life depended on it told me I hadn't been wrong about you. I couldn't swim out to you fast enough."

Her face glistened with moisture. "Are we through talking now?"

He chuckled. "Not yet, but soon. Let's get back to the house and relieve Cosimo. He deserves a break if Demi has fallen apart again. They all do."

A half hour later, Nik grasped her hand and they tiptoed into the nursery. Cosimo had dealt with a miserable Demi until they got there. Now they were finally alone with the baby, who'd fallen asleep.

He pulled Fran close. "Since the hospital in Leminos, I've had this dream we'd get married and adopt her. I honestly believe Melina made sure she was dropped literally at your feet so you'd become her new mother. That's why Demi reached out to you."

Fran hugged him with all the strength in her. "It felt like heaven had delivered her expressly to me."

"Then let's adopt her as our own miracle daughter and give her all the love we can. Later on we'll adopt another baby and another after that."

"You're making me too happy, Nik." She sobbed against his shoulder.

"We need to get married soon so she'll become bilingual in a hurry."

"I've got to learn Greek fast! Oh—I'll have to resign from my job at the hospital."

"We'll tell my parents in the morning." He rocked her in his arms for a long time. "I'm going to enjoy seeing the look in their eyes. They're not going to believe their youngest upstart son is finally going to settle down."

"They've had to wait a long time." She laughed through the tears. "Mine won't believe it either. They're going to adore you."

"You've already got my family wrapped around your little finger."

"It's you I'm worried about. Let's go in the bedroom so we won't wake up Demi."

He pulled her into the other room before cupping her face. "I want to spend the rest of the night with you, but I'm old-fashioned and would like your father's permission to marry you before I work my wicked ways with you. My bachelor days have come to an end. You're going to be my precious wife and I want to do everything right."

"You *do* do everything right. So right, I don't know how I was ever lucky enough to have found you. Just be with me for a little while. We'll stay dressed on top of the covers," she begged.

His lips twitched. "Once I start touching you, I'll never stop. I want you to be able to tell Kellie that I didn't coerce you into marrying me."

Her eyes filled again. "I wish I'd never told you anything about our conversation."

"Hush. I'm glad you did. Now we don't have any secrets. That's the way it should be. When you think Kellie's ready, you can tell her about our mutual problem."

"She'll be mortified when she learns what happened to you on that climb."

He smoothed the hair off her forehead. "But you'll know how to comfort her. She needs a lot of that right now while her marriage is suffering. That's one of your special gifts. Now kiss me like you mean it, then let me go for tonight. Tomorrow, and all the tomorrows after that, will be a different story."

"Nik—"

CHAPTER TEN

Three weeks later...

"Time for your nap, sweetheart." Demi had finished her lunch. Fran took her from the high chair and carried her through the penthouse to the bedroom they'd turned into a nursery filled with adorable baby furniture and curtains.

After changing her diaper, Fran put her down in the crib. She sang her one song. "Now be a good girl for Mommy and go to sleep. I've got a lot to do before your daddy gets home tonight."

Her watch said one-thirty. There was still the table to set in the dining area and the kitchen to clean up, not to mention making the bed and getting herself ready later. She'd bought a new black dress with spaghetti straps in the hope of wowing her new husband.

Today marked their first-week anniversary as man and wife. She was making some of Nik's favorite foods for a special dinner she wanted to be perfect. Fran had gotten the recipes from his mother and had already been on the phone with her twice to make sure she was doing the moussaka right.

The traditional recipe called for eggplant and meat

filling. "But the trick," his mother said, "is to layer in potatoes and zucchini to make it even richer before you top it with the bechamel sauce. Use heavy cream. My Nikki will love it."

Fran loved her new mother-in-law and smiled as she hurried back through the rooms to the kitchen. She hardly recognized Nik's elegant bachelor domicile anymore. The penthouse was still filled with light and open, but a family lived here now, complete with a baby. It contained the kind of clutter that turned a house into a home. She was so happy it was scary.

Today Nik had gone to the office for the first time. She'd missed him horribly.

Because of the baby, they hadn't taken an official honeymoon yet. In another month they hoped Demi would be able to handle a few days away from them, but none of it mattered. Once they'd said their vows at the chapel in Mykonos with their families looking on, they'd become insatiable lovers.

The only thing to mar the event was Kellie's absence. After she'd learned there was going to be a wedding, and had been told the true facts, she was desolate for all the things she'd said. But Nik had gotten on the phone and put her mind at ease. Just when Fran thought she couldn't love the man more, he did something to win her heart all over again.

Unfortunately, Kellie hadn't been feeling well and decided not to make the flight over.

Fran believed her, but she also knew she was afraid to come to Greece. Leandros kept an eye on her even when they were apart. He would know if she returned to attend the wedding. Fran promised to stay in close touch with her.

Nik had taken another week off in order to be home. When they weren't playing with the baby or eating, they found joy in each other's arms. Fran was existing on an entirely different level of happiness. It transcended what she'd known before.

The thought of tonight after they'd put the baby down and could concentrate on each other sent heat surging through her body. It was embarrassing how eager she was, but she loved her husband so much, she couldn't hide it if she tried.

She hurried into their bedroom barefooted to get busy and was just smoothing the duvet when she was grasped at the waist from behind and spun around.

"Nik!" she squealed in shock and joy. No one looked more gorgeous than he did, especially in his tan suit and tie. "You're not supposed to be home until tonight! You've caught me looking terrible."

His dark eyes devoured her. "Every husband should be so lucky to come home and find his wife in a pair of shorts like yours. I have to admit my T-shirt adds an allure, but I think we'll dispense with it."

"Darling," she half giggled the words as he put actions to his words and followed her down on top of the bed she'd just made.

"There's no help for you now," he growled the words into her neck. "I peeked in on Demi and she's out for the count."

"But today's your first day back."

"It was." He plundered her mouth until she was breathless. "Sandro told me I was worthless and sent me home."

"He didn't—"

Nik rolled her over so she was lying on top of him.

"No, he didn't. Actually, I sat at my desk and didn't hear a word my assistant said to me. My bros came in to eat lunch with me. When I couldn't carry on a coherent conversation with them, I knew what I had to do."

He turned her on her back once more. "Something smelled good when I walked in."

"It's my surprise dinner for you."

That heartbreaking smile broke out on his handsome face before he pulled a necklace out of his pocket. "This is a choker of gemstones the color of your eyes. It's for seven days of bliss," he murmured as he fastened it around her neck. "Happy anniversary, you beautiful creature. If a man could die from too much happiness, I'd have expired a week ago."

"I love you, Nik. I love you," she cried as rapture took over. She forgot everything until they heard Demi start to fuss much later.

Nik groaned and slowly relinquished her mouth with a smile. "We're going to have to do something about this. While I was in my office, the thought came to me that you could work with me. We'd bring in a playpen for Demi."

Laughter bubbled out of Fran. "That would be a novelty for about ten minutes before it turned into a disaster, but I love the idea of it. Maybe if your father put in two days a week, you and I would have more time together and could sail around the Aegean with our little girl. What do you think?"

He planted a long, hard kiss on her mouth. "I love the way you think. I'll call him later."

"Go ahead and do it right now. Think how happy it will make him."

Nik frowned. "What's the matter? Are you tired of me already?"

"Darling—" She leaned over him, kissing every centimeter of his face. "You know better than that. I just thought if you do this now, my Atlas will stop worrying about him. I'm afraid I'm very selfish and want all your thoughts centered on me."

"Don't you know they are?" he asked in a husky voice. "Why do you think I came home early today?"

She pressed a kiss to his lips. "Then humor me."

He groaned again. "Hand me your phone. Mine is on the floor with my clothes."

"Where they *should* be."

Laughter escaped his throat. "Whoever dreamed I'd be married to such a 'wicked' wife?"

"There's still a lot you don't know about me." With a chuckle, she took her phone from the bedside table.

As he pressed the digits, she whispered in his ear. "Tell him we need him to start work as soon as possible. I want you all to myself for as long as you can stand me. When the tornado brought Demi to me, it also brought her uncle. *It was written in the whirlwind.*"

* * * * *

Mills & Boon® Hardback

February 2013

ROMANCE

Sold to the Enemy	Sarah Morgan
Uncovering the Silveri Secret	Melanie Milburne
Bartering Her Innocence	Trish Morey
Dealing Her Final Card	Jennie Lucas
In the Heat of the Spotlight	Kate Hewitt
No More Sweet Surrender	Caitlin Crews
Pride After Her Fall	Lucy Ellis
Living the Charade	Michelle Conder
The Downfall of a Good Girl	Kimberly Lang
The One That Got Away	Kelly Hunter
Her Rocky Mountain Protector	Patricia Thayer
The Billionaire's Baby SOS	Susan Meier
Baby out of the Blue	Rebecca Winters
Ballroom to Bride and Groom	Kate Hardy
How To Get Over Your Ex	Nikki Logan
Must Like Kids	Jackie Braun
The Brooding Doc's Redemption	Kate Hardy
The Son that Changed his Life	Jennifer Taylor

MEDICAL

An Inescapable Temptation	Scarlet Wilson
Revealing The Real Dr Robinson	Dianne Drake
The Rebel and Miss Jones	Annie Claydon
Swallowbrook's Wedding of the Year	Abigail Gordon

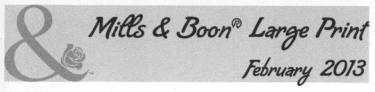

Mills & Boon® Large Print
February 2013

ROMANCE

HISTORICAL

MEDICAL

EN STD LP

Mills & Boon® Hardback
March 2013

ROMANCE

Playing the Dutiful Wife	Carol Marinelli
The Fallen Greek Bride	Jane Porter
A Scandal, a Secret, a Baby	Sharon Kendrick
The Notorious Gabriel Diaz	Cathy Williams
A Reputation For Revenge	Jennie Lucas
Captive in the Spotlight	Annie West
Taming the Last Acosta	Susan Stephens
Island of Secrets	Robyn Donald
The Taming of a Wild Child	Kimberly Lang
First Time For Everything	Aimee Carson
Guardian to the Heiress	Margaret Way
Little Cowgirl on His Doorstep	Donna Alward
Mission: Soldier to Daddy	Soraya Lane
Winning Back His Wife	Melissa McClone
The Guy To Be Seen With	Fiona Harper
Why Resist a Rebel?	Leah Ashton
Sydney Harbour Hospital: Evie's Bombshell	Amy Andrews
The Prince Who Charmed Her	Fiona McArthur

MEDICAL

NYC Angels: Redeeming The Playboy	Carol Marinelli
NYC Angels: Heiress's Baby Scandal	Janice Lynn
St Piran's: The Wedding!	Alison Roberts
His Hidden American Beauty	Connie Cox

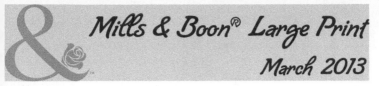

Mills & Boon® Large Print
March 2013

ROMANCE

A Night of No Return	Sarah Morgan
A Tempestuous Temptation	Cathy Williams
Back in the Headlines	Sharon Kendrick
A Taste of the Untamed	Susan Stephens
The Count's Christmas Baby	Rebecca Winters
His Larkville Cinderella	Melissa McClone
The Nanny Who Saved Christmas	Michelle Douglas
Snowed in at the Ranch	Cara Colter
Exquisite Revenge	Abby Green
Beneath the Veil of Paradise	Kate Hewitt
Surrendering All But Her Heart	Melanie Milburne

HISTORICAL

How to Sin Successfully	Bronwyn Scott
Hattie Wilkinson Meets Her Match	Michelle Styles
The Captain's Kidnapped Beauty	Mary Nichols
The Admiral's Penniless Bride	Carla Kelly
Return of the Border Warrior	Blythe Gifford

MEDICAL

Her Motherhood Wish	Anne Fraser
A Bond Between Strangers	Scarlet Wilson
Once a Playboy…	Kate Hardy
Challenging the Nurse's Rules	Janice Lynn
The Sheikh and the Surrogate Mum	Meredith Webber
Tamed by her Brooding Boss	Joanna Neil